Recovering Charles

OTHER BOOKS BY JASON F. WRIGHT

Christmas Jars

The Wednesday Letters

Recovering Charles

A NOVEL BY

JASON F. WRIGHT

SHADOW
MOUNTAIN

To Kodi

I'd swim through a hurricane for you

"Love Me if You Can" music and lyrics by Cherie Call © 2008 Mendonhouse Music (ASCAP). Used by permission. http://www.cheriecall.com

© 2008 Jason F. Wright

Visit us at ShadowMountain.com

Library of Congress Cataloging-in-Publication Data

Wright, Jason F.
　　Recovering Charles / Jason F. Wright.
　　　　p.　cm.
　　ISBN 978-1-59038-964-5 (alk. paper)
　　1. Fathers and sons—Fiction.　2. Adult children—Fiction.　3. New Orleans (La.)—Fiction.　I. Title.
　　PS3623.R539R43 2008
　　813'.6—dc22　　　　　　　　　　　　　　　　　　　　　　2008018859

Printed in the United States of America
R. R. Donnelley and Sons, Crawfordsville, IN

10　9　8　7　6　5　4　3　2　1

PROLOGUE

Present Day

I can't look up without seeing it.

But it's not there by chance. It's precisely centered on the wall opposite my desk. Blown up in black and white. I cannot escape it. Framed in imported Japanese wood more expensive than the laptop I use to write my story. It's just one of the thousands of pictures I've taken in the last decade. Maybe hundreds of thousands.

But only one hangs on the wall facing my desk.

A small, faceless crowd at a distance. A figure on a nearby sidewalk dressed in a white suit. A plain wooden casket with only a few flowers. Two men playing saxophone, one more on trumpet, one on trombone. One woman singing at the front of the marching caravan, one more twirling a parasol, and two more simply following along.

In a life tattooed by mistakes and heartache, both inflicted and received, the photo symbolizes my most treasured accomplishment and the anguish it caused me.

And it means more to me than the Pulitzer it won.

♩♩♩

Charles Millward was born a brilliant musician.

Not exactly a brilliant *player* of music, but a remarkable musician all the same. He once told Mr. Dalton's fifth grade class on Parents' Day that if you listed America's top ten thousand saxophone players he wouldn't make the list.

"Now kids, if the list *only* includes men who play the sax, and *only* men born in January, and *only* those with four smelly toes on their left foot because the fifth never popped out while I was cooking in Luke's grandma's belly, then I *might* make the list . . ."

The kids laughed.

"But," Dad added, "*only* if you made it the top ten thousand *and one.*"

The kids laughed even harder, and I grinned in the big cheesy way that only a 5th grader totally enamored with his father can.

Then came Dad's punch line. "And I'm the *and one.*"

No, Dad's fat, clumsy fingers didn't love the sax as much as his heart ever did. In college he was self-taught on guitar and could find his way around almost any instrument. And though he became quite good on the piano, enough so he could survive on tips at local bars, I think his soul loved playing the sax most.

He heard music when others didn't. We learned through the years that Dad even *thought* in musical notes. Mom said he spoke that way too, in meter, with an ebb and flow, pausing, building strength, a crescendo, a long finish. A deep breath.

I always wondered if he read music the way I looked at photos, or like Pavarotti sang, Michelangelo sculpted, or Orson Welles made movies. Even as a child I remember noticing Dad's eyes dance from note to note as he played the songs he had scribbled in a ragged leather journal held together by two fat rubber bands.

Sometimes at night he'd bring in his journal and his guitar and play me a song at the foot of my bed. The sax was his most prized possession, though his Gibson acoustic wasn't far behind. I didn't care that his voice would often crack and fall. The melodies sold the songs.

"Every note tells a song's story," Dad liked to say. "And every song, no matter how short, has a second verse. You just have to find it."

It took me a long time to learn what Dad meant. I don't think Mom ever did.

Still, I do think she loved my father.

Except when she was high.

The doctor first prescribed sleeping pills for my mother in June of 1990.

They worked.

Mother slept through the rising temperatures of Fort Worth, Texas, through our cul-de-sac's Fourth of July celebration, and into the dog days of August.

The country prepared for war in Iraq.

Dad watched.

Mom slept.

And Dad never left her side. Not when his job at one of the country's top architectural firms was threatened. Not when the sleeping pills didn't satisfy her anymore and he discovered Vicodin in an Advil bottle on her nightstand. Not even when she begged him to take me far away and let her fade from this life.

"I won't," he said.

My father clung to his complicated, braided rope of faith. He said one day Mother's soul would surface again and she'd return to the elementary school and the students she once loved.

The girls made her construction-paper cards with white tissue-paper flowers glued to the front. The boys made cards, too, adorned with blue Dallas Cowboy stars and football helmets.

Everyone missed Mrs. Millward.

But no one ached for her like Dad.

I've seen every Sunday night, inspirational made-for-TV movie where towering heroes in death's grasp never give up their positive attitudes. They somehow muster the strength to encourage others to love more, to forgive, to live their lives better. Jack

Lemmon died that way in *Tuesdays with Morrie,* so did Ronald Reagan playing Gipp in *Knute Rockne: All American.*

Optimism. Spirit. Readiness for whatever hides just beyond the light.

I wish that had been Mom. Just one year after Grandma's accident, Mom took every pill she could find, including some Dad had locked in his den, and took a nap she hoped would be her last.

Dad found her dead in their bed.

Her head was under her pillow, hiding from the world even at the very end.

She left the world bitter and cursing. She cursed the pharmaceutical companies for making the drugs that stole her will. She cursed the doctors she'd begged to prescribe them. She cursed God for making her dependent on pills. She even cursed Dad for not leaving and making a better life for the two of us.

Mom died hating her husband and his premonitions, hating the rain, Mexicans, the sun, her therapist, mornings, Sundays, Barbara Walters, and sometimes me.

But mostly I think she just hated God.

Four days later, at her funeral, a dozen mourners passed by her casket and whispered good-byes and condolences. They thought she looked at peace. So warm and restful.

I thought she looked every bit as cold as she had the last year of her life.

I'll never forget Dad's unfinished eulogy. His voice cracked as he began reading the lyrics to a song he'd written for Mom during their courtship. He made eye contact with me and began to weep. He covered his eyes with one hand and pounded the other on the pulpit so hard it tipped to the right and almost toppled. His word-for-word remarks, scribbled on white 5x7 cards, scattered on the floor.

Dad's best friend, Kaiser, a man he'd worked with side by side at their firm, gathered up the cards, put them back in order, and finished the eulogy.

Kaiser read about Mom and Dad's first meeting at a science fair in high school, about Dad's premonitions, their joy at my birth, the hole in his heart that wouldn't be healed until he saw her in the house he'd some day build for them in heaven.

When Kaiser finished, he set the cards aside and added some impromptu words of his own. He thanked my father for his years of friendship and pledged to stand by him the way Dad had stood by Kaiser during some challenging times of his own.

"Ladies and gentlemen, Charles Millward has been there for all of us. He was there for me when I almost lost my job a few years back. He defended my honor when others at work wouldn't. There's no other way to say it, he saved my bacon." Kaiser pulled a handkerchief from his pocket and blew his nose hard three times, getting louder with each honk.

Someone's little boy in the back row giggled before his mother's hand clamped across his mouth.

"You all know it's true," Kaiser continued. "Charlie would walk to the end of the longest road in Texas to help anyone here. He was there for his wife when life got so hard none of us could imagine it. It wasn't easy for Charles to watch his dream girl, his one true love, struggle through this last year. But he was there no matter what." Kaiser looked at Dad and seemed to wait until the rest of us were looking at him, too. "Now it's our turn to be there for him."

Dad slumped into the chair next to me on the front row, and I draped my arm awkwardly around him. His body shook.

I cried, too, but mostly for Dad.

The next decade and a half passed by like a Texas thunderstorm. Lightning quick. Not enough rain.

Today is like any other in our microscopic Manhattan studio apartment. I'm alone. Around me and within easy reach are my four angels: my 35-millimeter old-school camera (a Canon EOS 1v), a ridiculously expensive digital (a Canon 5D), my baby (a MacBook Pro), and my sweet Jesse (a saxophone).

Meanwhile, my real-live angel is almost certainly sitting at her City Hall desk arguing with her cubical-mate about Barry Bonds and Roger Clemens or last year's World Series. In between rounds they will cooperate long enough to write grants and chase music education funding for the city's more than six hundred elementary schools. She will twist arms, use more salt than sugar, offer to pick up a check personally at their home if necessary, insist on e-mailing an MP3 file of a recent concert at the Brooklyn Music School.

She's not trained in this field, but she's become an expert anyway. And she'll win. She always wins.

Tonight at home she'll playfully gloat and tease me about my desk. It's an organized mess. Invoices, photos, proof sheets, and catalogues sit in staggered stacks near the back edge in a line. They hang an inch off the edge, daring my feet to kick them to the floor like heavy broken parachutes for the second time this afternoon.

I'll remind her of my favorite NYU professor's theory: Desks were made for propping up feet. Most of Larry's lectures were given from his squeaky chair at the front of the mini-auditorium, and his feet, shoeless but always hidden in navy blue dress socks, rested on the front edge of his desk as he lounged backward.

Larry is a good man. It's no stretch to say I learned everything I know about the eternally intimate relationship between life and the lens from that man. That was his phrase, "eternally intimate."

"Luke Millward owes his career to Larry Gorton." At least that's what my colleagues say when they see my work in *National Geographic, Time,* or on the front page of a top-fifty newspaper. They're right.

After all, Larry's the one who talked me into going to New Orleans.

PART 1

CHAPTER

1

Monday, August 29, 2005

New Orleans was underwater.

The storm had come; the one the Gulf had always feared. Hurricane Katrina brushed Florida as a Category 1, killing eleven and leaving a million in the dark. Then it strengthened over the ocean and made landfall twice more, unleashing its fury on the Gulf Coast like a woman scorned. No mercy. Thousands fled before impact; thousands more stayed.

The footage was numbing.

Fats Domino was reported missing. So, too, were countless other musicians who had built the city but whose names we wouldn't know.

The French Quarter was mostly spared the flooding, but blocks away the water had baptized homes, businesses, nightclubs, and the homeless.

Fox News' Shepard Smith was standing on Canal Street. He tossed the segment to an unrecognizable reporter three miles away who was on a small fishing boat in the Lower Ninth Ward. The reporter gestured to a body twenty feet away—facedown, arms and legs spread out, like an upside-down snow angel. "It's hard to imagine what these people endured in their final moments. Impossible. Back to you, Shep."

Cameras captured water gushing over one levee while a helicopter dropped giant sandbags on a gaping hole in another.

A dozen residents stood on the roof of a fourplex apartment building. They'd made a cross with paper towels. A voice described what we so clearly saw for ourselves and asked viewers to imagine what it must feel like to sit so helpless on an island.

A mother nursed her baby under the privacy of a brown bath towel, and we wondered how long her milk would last without food or clean water.

Every channel had the same images. They came from slightly different views and were painted with their own set of dramatic adjectives. But the images were the same.

A man named Bernard was wading to the Superdome.

Bernard's wife, Donna, was missing. Seventy-one years old. She had gone to check on their daughter and her two grandbabies a few blocks away. He hadn't seen her since the levees broke. She needed her heart medication and would die without it.

"Anyone watching, anyone, please, anyone watching, please watch out for my Donna. And pray, please, that she's waiting for me on dry ground."

I didn't remember praying since 2002 when turbulence tossed my plane around before landing in Salt Lake City for the Winter Games. I closed my eyes and began to whisper.

My cell phone rang.

FOUNTAIN REALTY

Jordan Knapp was the best friend I'd ever had. And she also happened to be the most beautiful.

She was confident but self-aware, and never condescending. Average height. Natural blonde hair that seemed to grow an inch every time I saw her. Real. Reliable. A problem solver. A Realtor. One of the most talented guitar players I'd ever known. A textbook self-starter. Punctual.

Always punctual.

"Hey, Luke."

"Hey, Jordan."

"Just got a contract on the place in midtown. The condo."

"Toldja you would." I flipped back to Fox from CNN.

"Yes, you did. Let's celebrate over Italian food tonight?"

"Sure."

"I'll be at your place at seven. Cab to Little Italy?"

"Seven."

"Something wrong?"

"Nah."

"Luuukey."

"Jooordy." Punctual *and* perceptive.

"What's up, Luke? What's going on?"

"We'll talk tonight," I said, watching the flickering images and listening to a reporter describe why some doors already had white X's and others didn't. *Dead bodies.*

"Good. See you at seven."

It was no secret that when Jordan closed her eyes, she saw a classic Disney prince and princess romance in our future. But that future for me hadn't arrived yet, and I wondered if it ever would. I loved her, certainly, but mostly I loved knowing that this was the most useful relationship I'd ever had. Where she saw a spring wedding and her mother's pearl-white wedding dress, I saw the next movie, ball game, dinner out, or daytrip to the country.

♩♩♩

Jordan and I met at NYU. She'd been a law student; I was studying photojournalism.

We met at a birthday party for someone neither of us knew, and we clicked. She was a willing ear, an attractive one, sure, but we hadn't noticed each other romantically. At least I hadn't. In time she became bored with law school and earned her real-estate license.

We hadn't crossed paths for almost six months until a chance encounter at a club in Atlantic City where we discussed organized religion, relationships, Wendy's fries versus McDonald's fries, and the career ladder for detectives.

"Luke, listen to me again, it goes like this."

Eye-rolling.

She laughed. "Seriously, it goes like this. A Sleuth is the highest you can get. It goes Private Eye, then Junior Detective, then Detective—like if you go to school or the police academy for a diploma. Then if you're top-notch, I mean the *best*, and your peers recognize you that way, you become a Sleuth."

"Sleuth."

"That's what I said. Sleuth."

More eye-rolling.

"OK, OK," she continued. "Think about *Magnum P.I.* Tom Selleck played a private investigator, a good one mind you, and de-li-cious on the eyes, but he wasn't a detective because he didn't have the piece of paper or formal training."

Now I added laughter to the eye-rolling. "You've lost it, Jordan. You've jumped the shark this time."

"So in closing . . ." She flipped her hair and acted as if she hadn't heard me.

I liked it.

"The tasty Tom Selleck could never become an *actual* Sleuth, because he didn't have enough respect from his peers. He was too much a renegade. You need industry support to reach—"

"All right! I give, Matlock!"

"Now *that* guy could have been a Sleuth—"

"You win!"

"It took you long enough." She pulled her hair toward her right side, draping it over her shoulder, and let linger a style of smile that I'd never seen from her before. Seductive. Soft. "I hope it doesn't take you that long to ask me out."

Why not? I thought.

We left the club and I bought her a strawberry-topped Belgian waffle at an IHOP in Jersey.

"Make a bet?" she asked.

"OK. I'll bite."

"If I can eat this waffle in five minutes or less you have to take me to any restaurant I want for our first *real* date."

"How about three?" I countered.

"Four."

"Deal. And if you *can't* eat that ginormous waffle in four minutes or less?"

"I'll teach you to play the acoustic as well as I can."

"Chomp chomp!" I taunted.

Two weeks later we ate at the Rainbow Room in the RCA building. The meal was so expensive I could have paid for personal lessons from Eric Clapton.

That was the night I expected the spark my father had described to ignite my heart and change the nature of our friendship.

It didn't, though I held hope it someday would.

CHAPTER

2

I couldn't turn off the TV.

I had plenty to do the week Katrina rearranged the Gulf. I was on deadlines to deliver photos to two clients and was already a week late on delivering a rough cut of a DVD slideshow I'd created for Jordan's real-estate broker.

But I just couldn't turn it off.

The final death toll would be hard to pin down, Louisiana Governor Kathleen Blanco said in a news conference. She was taking a beating from the national press, which some felt was unfair. Mayor Ray Nagin also had his critics for what they called his dramatic exaggerations and tendency to place blame everywhere except on his own shoulders. Images of submerged and abandoned yellow school buses filled TV screens and newspaper front pages. But above all, FEMA had become the easiest target. Federal bureaucracy. Washington, D.C. mentality. A useless Bush crony. A disconnected president.

None of that mattered to me. Not as I heard another explanation of how the levees failed and Lake Pontchartrain had taken eighty percent of the city prisoner. Not as I watched a woman sob on live national TV that her twin sons were missing. Nine years old. Former Haitian refugees. One was wearing a red tank top and the other his favorite New Orleans Saints T-shirt.

I'd never felt such raw emotion for anyone not sharing my last name.

I changed the channel. Bernard was on another network. He had arrived at the Superdome but had yet to find his wife. He carried a wallet-sized picture of her. He was drinking a Dasani.

"Good, someone got him water. Keep looking, Bernard, you'll find her." I didn't mean to say any of that out loud, but I did.

I flipped to MSNBC. They reminded us the hurricane hadn't only been cruel to New Orleans. For half an hour, local NBC reporters in Florida, Alabama, and Mississippi went national to tell their stories. Hellacious devastation in Long Beach, Mississippi. Power outages in Mobile, Alabama. Fires everywhere. Hospitals shuttling patients out of state. Neighbors helping neighbors.

I opened my laptop and visited the Red Cross web site. I donated a hundred dollars to their Katrina Disaster Relief Fund and bookmarked the page.

I turned the television channel again. An unknown but attractive, well-groomed female reporter was outside giving an update on the state of the Superdome. The sun was beating down on those camped along the sidewalk and cries could be heard all around her.

In the background, a black man knelt over a body covered from the neck down with a gray bedsheet. He pulled the sheet over the body's head and turned toward the camera, screaming in agony.

Bernard.

Tears began to drop for a man I'd never meet face-to-face and for the woman he loved.

I found yet another channel offering wall-to-wall coverage, but I don't remember which. They were showing a series of still shots set to a slickly produced dramatic soundtrack—

A body in a grassy median, covered with a stunningly vibrant American flag.

National Guard troops on helicopters.

The roof of the Superdome. Most of its tiles ripped in half or missing completely. The building best suited to handle high winds in all the Crescent City in trouble. *Bitterly ironic,* I thought. *Water is leaking in. Hope is flooding out.*

Mississippi Governor Haley Barbour hugs a woman outside a temporary shelter.

Mormon missionaries hand out cases of water in a church parking lot.

A man and a teenager paddle three young children down a

street in a canoe. A fire burns behind them in an upscale neighborhood.

Cars stuck in an alley, buried under ten feet of water. They look like colored marbles at the bottom of a mud puddle.

A young, tall black man pushes a dead woman—probably his mother—in a wheelchair.

A red Chevy Cavalier sits in a hotel swimming pool.

A man sits alone on an overpass, clutching a black case. *I wonder if it's a saxophone.*

I was fourteen and certainly not the most popular kid in Mrs. Ingham's eighth grade music class. Everyone else had no trouble picking an instrument during the first week. We spent two days goofing around on twenty-year-old trombones, trumpets, clarinets, and whatever else Mrs. Ingham pulled from a closet in the back of the band room.

Wednesday was decision day.

"Can I pick last?" I'd always known I'd go with whatever Chrissy Alves picked. She'd never even *looked* at me before, but playing the same instrument might finally be the excuse I needed to say hello or punch her in the arm the way other boys did to the girls they liked.

Mrs. Ingham smiled warmly. "I suppose, Luke."

One by one the other kids announced their choices. Big

Spencer chose the bass drum. No surprise there, not with the way he liked beating up on people. Olivia chose the violin because she already owned one and had taken a few private lessons. Our popular eighth grade class president, Matthew, went with the tuba, and Green Beret-bound Glen chose the trumpet. His best friend Bryan went for the tambourine on the theory it would give him the greatest opportunity to sleep during class. Caleb only wanted to sing, and quite loudly, but Mrs. Ingham made him pick an instrument anyway.

"But my voice *is* an instrument," Caleb argued.

"I know, Caleb, and a finely-tuned instrument it is, but chorus doesn't start until next semester. So choose a musical instrument, please."

He went for the cymbals and played them with gusto.

The Wages twins picked saxophones. Jay had really wanted to play the bassoon but the school didn't own one. He settled for the trombone. The new girl from Minnesota picked an orange-colored French horn that was already bent.

Then came Chrissy. She sat at the end of the row below me; I was perched alone on the highest riser. I looked at her profile and admired her sparkly purple hairband. I prayed, *Please don't pick the—*

"Flute!" she announced proudly.

Mrs. Ingham smiled toward me again. She clearly enjoyed this. "And last but not least, how about you up there at the top?

Mr. Millward? The flute for you as well?" She winked. I hated it when teachers winked.

The boys giggled and Spencer practically screamed, "You two will make *beautiful* music together."

Now the girls giggled, too. I might have slugged Spencer if he hadn't already locked me in the custodial closet twice that year.

Mrs. Ingham disappeared into the deep closet and came out with two tarnished silver flutes and two different-sized cases. "Here you go, you two." She surveyed the class, each of us awkwardly handling our instruments and making sounds normally heard in emergency rooms and jungles. "And now we have a band!"

Over the next two weeks we learned fingering and then, finally, scales. After another month of screeching out music that Mrs. Ingham called "beautiful," we learned a John Philips Sousa song that would have been unrecognizable to Mr. Sousa himself.

"It's time to practice on your own, students. This is what eighth grade is all about. Responsibility. If we want to be ready for the afternoon concert next month, you'll have to commit to practicing outside of class."

I hated practicing the flute at home almost as much as I hated blowing on the thing *during* class. But the flute kept me four inches closer to Chrissy Alves on the front row. Sometimes when she played, and she'd actually gotten pretty good, I would only *pretend* to play so I could look at her puckered lips through the corner of my eye. I secretly hoped she'd never been kissed and that I'd be her first, but I was afraid I was too late. The rumors were that she'd gone behind the school's landscaping shed last year and left the Virgin Lips Club with a boy nicknamed "Funk," kissing him square on the mouth. For obvious reasons, she denied it. But the silly look on Funk's tomato-face whenever she looked at him gave it away.

"Are you all listening to me?" We packed up our instruments and shoved sheet music we didn't really understand into our backpacks. "Practice this weekend, please. I expect to be emotionally moved by your progress on Monday."

I took a deep breath and punched Chrissy in the arm.

"Hi, Chrissy."

"Hi, Luke."

"You gonna be practicing this weekend?"

"I guess I better after *that* speech." She grinned and pulled grape lip gloss from the pencil pocket of her purple backpack.

Is she going to put that on right in front of me?

Gulp. She did.

"That's awesome. I like practicing, too. A lot, too."

"That's good." She put the lip gloss away and rubbed her lips together.

"Would you like to, ah, to practice playing the flutes with me?" *Flutes?*

She studied my face for what felt like hours. By the time she spoke, I was so shaky I needed the boys' bathroom. I tried not to squirm and almost teared up at the thought of wetting my pants in front of the prettiest girl in the eighth grade.

"Sure, I'll practice playing the *flutes* with you." Her bright eyes could light a fire.

I nodded. Words couldn't have escaped my cotton mouth even if I'd tried.

"You know where I live?"

I shook my head no. A big fat lie.

"I live across from the Kimbles. On Reservoir Road."

"Oh, yeah," I croaked. "Knew that."

"Come over Sunday after church. We get home at 12:15 or so."

"Awesome." I picked up my backpack and casually threw it over one shoulder.

"Don't forget your flute," she said.

"Yeah, duh." I reached back down, grabbed the case, and unzipped my backpack just enough to cram it inside.

"See you Sunday," she said, walking away.

"Awesome."

I practiced so much on Saturday that my lips were worn out from holding them in a position that should be reserved for first kisses. My hands ached and my pinkies were so sore I wanted to lop off them off with wire cutters. Dad came in every now and again to encourage me and to offer help. He took my flute and played a few bars.

"Geez, Dad, you play the flute, *too?*"

"Not really, but I know a *little* about a lot of instruments."

"I wish I'd picked something else." So did my pinkies.

"Don't say that, son. The flute is beautiful when played well. It's magical in fact. You'll get there."

"You don't wish I'd picked the sax?"

"Not at all. You have your reasons." He tapped my shin with his foot.

How does he know this stuff? I thought.

"Don't worry, Luke. Give it time, you'll get there."

"I doubt it."

Dad handed the flute back to me. "You made a brave choice, son. Stick with it. It will be worth it later."

Like tomorrow.

Just after noon the next day I threw my freshly-polished flute in my backpack and rode my black Huffy to Chrissy's house. She invited me in and led me to the living room where she'd already set up a folding music stand in front of two dining room chairs. She'd also arranged a TV tray with two glasses of Kool-Aid.

"Hope you like grape."

It could have been diesel fuel and I would have enjoyed it.

We sat side by side and blew our way through scales and then the only song we'd learned. We played it four or five times. Each time we'd start again her knee would inch closer to mine. By the time they touched I could barely breathe, never mind play the flute.

"You quit playing!" she squealed after the final note.

"Sorry." My heart was racing so fast I was sure she could hear it. "I lost my place." I pretended to straighten my sheet of paper on the stand we shared.

"You're funny, Luke Millward."

"You too." I turned to look at her and her nose was so close I felt her breath on my face. She was making the face she made just before putting the flute to her gloriously shiny lips. But the flute was still in her lap.

I leaned in and at last forfeited my membership in the VLC. That was the last thing I remember about the first time I practiced the flute with Chrissy Alves.

♩♩♩

Our Sunday practices became the highlight of my middle school musical career. I got exactly one kiss every time we practiced. It always went down on her terms and the timing was completely unexpected. I tried in vain to convince Chrissy we needed to practice on Saturdays, too.

Six kisses into our flute relationship, Mom and Dad made me invite her to our house for lunch and a practice session in Dad's den.

"We just want to meet your practice partner," Mom said.

"Fine. But you better buy some grape Kool-Aid."

Chrissy showed up the next Sunday afternoon and Dad led us into his den. We played our scales to his great satisfaction. Mom watched from the doorway.

"Outstanding, guys!" he said. "You sound great! Really good work. How about you play something from the concert coming up?"

We played one of the three songs we'd learned. I'd played them so many times I didn't even read the sheet music anymore. Dad praised us again and excused himself. He left the door open.

Chrissy and I played through each song one more time before taking a break to drink our Kool-Aid.

"What's your dad's job?" Chrissy asked.

"He's an architect."

"Like Mr. Brady!"

"You got it!" If she thought she was clever, I thought she was clever, too.

"So he builds buildings. That's a cool job."

"I guess. He doesn't really build 'em, I don't think, more like draws them out. Then like a million people look at them and say it's OK to actually build it. Dad's always talking about red tape." I sat a little straighter. "Red tape means all the—"

"I know what it means, Luke."

"Yeah, figured you did." I slumped.

We finished off our Kool-Aid.

Chrissy gestured with one hand while wiping her purple mustache with the other. "What's in there?" She'd spotted Dad's saxophone case on the bottom shelf of the bookcase.

"That's nothing, just my dad's old sax." Shortening it made me feel like a high schooler.

"Can I see it?"

"Better not, it's super expensive. I'm not allowed to even carry the case for him. He's had it since he got married. Mom bought it for him for their first Christmas. I could tell you the story, I've heard it a billion times."

"That's OK. Sorry for asking." She took another sip and looked embarrassed for bringing it up.

Thinking first was never my strong suit. "Hold on." I put my flute on my chair and walked over to the open door. I peeked out then pulled it shut. I carefully opened the case and pulled the heavy saxophone from its red felt bed. It was even heavier than I'd expected. I carried it across the room and placed it in her hands.

"Wow, Luke. This is *so* nice. It's so beautiful compared to the ones at school. It weighs like a hundred pounds. It must have cost a fortune, huh?"

"Definitely." *Hey, she thinks we're rich!* I wiped my palms on my jeans. "Better get it back."

"Yeah, you better." She handed it to me and I turned back toward the case. Only I hadn't realized how close I'd gotten to

Dad's heavy music stand and my left foot tripped over one of the legs. The stand fell and Chrissy yelped.

I fell too. Right on top of Dad's saxophone.

Before I'd even turned over, Dad had flung the door open and rushed over to me.

He scooped up the instrument.

"Luke Millward! What did you do? What happened here?" Dad spun the saxophone end-to-end, examining the neck, mouthpiece, and rods.

I noticed the small indentation in the bell the same time he did.

I couldn't speak.

Chrissy was frantically packing her flute.

"Luke!" Dad barked.

"Sorry." I looked at my feet. "We were just—"

"Just what? Disobeying me? Showing off for your girlfriend? Which was it?"

"Dad—"

"Well? Now you've damaged the instrument. Do you have *any* idea what this means to me? Your mother saved like a pauper to buy this for me."

"I said I was sorry."

Chrissy also mumbled a "Sorry" and a "Good-bye, Luke" and scampered out the door.

Good-bye indeed. She never spoke to me again.

CHAPTER

3

S ix o'clock AM.

The TV was on again.

A reporter at the Convention Center described terror overnight in a bathroom. A rape. A knife attack. Mayhem as refugees battled for water and a cot. Circumstances at the Superdome weren't much better, warned another reporter.

Gunfire peppered the air from underneath an overpass. A pickup raced away with a man standing in the bed of the truck, holding a roll bar with one hand and a gun with the other. An eyewitness used the third *Mad Max* reference of the day.

The fierce debates over the government's response continued. There were more facts in dispute than agreement. But one truth permeated the Gulf: people were suffering.

The "city in a bowl" was drowning.

I didn't sleep much that week. Katrina's images and the evolving stories of heartache and heroism spun nonstop through my head. Experts warned it could be the end of October before the city was dry. Somehow the "Army Corp of Engineers" was becoming a household name.

The economic numbers were so staggering they didn't seem like numbers anymore. Damages topped $125 billion, five times what Hurricane Andrew cost South Florida. Insurance companies were already educating survivors on the difference between coverage for floods and coverage for hurricanes. With fanfare, FEMA was promising preloaded debit cards for everyone, a program that barely lasted long enough for a single visit to Home Depot.

I went back to the Red Cross web site and donated another two hundred dollars.

CNN was replaying snippets of a press conference. A FEMA spokesman was debunking the Convention Center rumors: no rapes. No murders. No anarchy. Later we'd learn the truth was somewhere in the middle. Yes, there had been anarchy, an understandable battle for survival that would have unfolded in any city in the world under similar circumstances. Yes, there were dead bodies and murder, but more of the former and fewer of the latter. In fact, only a few cases of homicide were confirmed.

Houston had begun receiving evacuees by the thousands, almost five hundred buses made the trek west on I-10. Others went north. Most of those who sought refuge at the airport weren't told where they were going until the planes touched down— Atlanta, Washington, D.C., Phoenix.

I wondered if the families, many of them permanently incomplete, would ever again see their beloved Big Easy. Would they cram into small spaces between tourists to watch the Zulu parade during Mardi Gras? Listen to jazz in the French Quarter? Watch the bucket drummer perform a one-handed drum roll at the corner of Bourbon and Toulouse?

I also wondered where my father was living.

Does he even know who Katrina is?

♩♩♩

Dad and I had last spoken sometime during the summer of 2003. He called from a pay phone in Austin, Texas, outside the Alamo Drafthouse. He was broke. Again. The script was familiar.

"Hi, son."

"Hello, Dad."

"How are you?"

"What do you need?"

"I asked how you were."

"I'm fine, Dad. What's up?"

"You ever been here? Austin?"

"You're back in Texas?"

"It's an amazing city, Luke. Come visit your dad this weekend."

Some nerve, I thought. "What happened to LA?"

"It wasn't for me."

Code for, "I ran out of money."

"Have you found a real job yet?" I stuck to the script.

"I'm looking. It's not easy for me. Not at my age."

Age is the least of your concerns.

"How about you? How's the photography? I always check the photo credits when I pick up a paper. Even saw the one in *Newsweek* of Hillary at the Yanks game. Great shot."

I would never admit to him that I'd wondered if he'd seen that particular photo. It had been a welcome boost to my career.

"Guess who bought me dinner a few weeks ago?" Dad asked.

"Kaiser."

"How'd you know?"

"Lucky guess," I said. *Who else would still buy you dinner?*

"He was in LA. Hadn't seen him in two or three years. Had a good time."

"I'm glad. He's a good man."

"The best," Dad said, then fell quiet. "Hey," he picked up a moment later, "you remember that summer that you, me, and Mom drove—"

"Yeah, Dad, I remember."

"Great summer. Really great summer . . . You still dating that girl from Mexico City?"

"No, Dad. That was three relationships ago."

"Oh . . . Sorry then."

"No need."

"Anyone new? You serious with anyone?"

"No."

Enough time passed without another question that even *I* became uncomfortable.

"Maybe it's time, son. Time to find someone special. A girl-friend who can become a wife. Someone like your mother was when she and I got married . . ."

His voice fell and I knew his mind was wandering. I knew he was drunk, though most people wouldn't have caught on. He'd become very adept at functioning while intoxicated.

"What's in Austin, Dad?"

"Music, son." His mood lightened instantly. "I followed it here. It's really something. Come on down and see your old man. I'm in the heart of this place. Heard of the Drafthouse Cinema? Famous, great character, great movies. Hop on a—"

"You know I can't." *More like I won't,* I admitted to myself.

"Can't or won't?" Dad asked.

Exactly.

"Maybe some other time." His voice darkened again.

Why bother? Next time you call you'll be in San Antonio or St. Louis or Miami.

"What's your One Good Thing today?"

I paused. I hadn't been asked that in years.

"I haven't had one yet," I said.

"Mine is right now. Talking to you. This is the best O.G.T. I've had in an awfully long time."

"That's nice." I was done with small talk. "Do you need money?" I counted six seconds tick off in silence.

"If you could."

"How much?"

"Whatever you can send—"

"How much?"

"Couple thousand?"

Rent or debts? I wondered. "Five hundred."

"That's perfect." A few beats. "I hate to even ask. You know, I've been eating leftovers from the kitchen here the last few nights. Staying on the couch of the drummer at—"

"Was it hard last time you called? Where was that—West Hollywood, right? You asked for twelve hundred that time."

"Luke. I'm trying. You *know* I'm trying."

"Trying what?" I knew.

"To dry out."

He'd been *trying* since his inappropriate dance with an ice sculpture atop the hors d'oeuvre table at his firm's open house barely a month after Mom died. In a catastrophic collapse he went from a social drinker to someone who couldn't have smelled worse if he ran moonshine.

"I'm trying," Dad repeated.

"I'm sure you are."

"I am, Luke. I'm getting there. I'm playing at a club. I only got here two weeks ago and I already got a regular gig with a local band. College kids. Talented kids, Luke. Really talented. We're playing Friday and Saturday nights. They start paying me my share this weekend. Playing mostly guitar . . . Miss the sax though."

"You're a middle-aged man playing in a band with college kids? That should sober you up." Cheap shots: my specialty when it came to my father.

"I said I'm trying."

"Great? How's A.A. then?"

"Actually I'm looking for a new sponsor right now. But I haven't had a drink—"

"Look, Dad, I really need to get going. Anything else?" I decided to make him ask again.

He took a few audible breaths. "You'll send the five hundred then?"

"Western Union."

"Thank you. There's one about two blocks—"

"Got it. I'll find it online." Then I repeated what I said every time this call came, though this time I hoped to actually mean it. "This is it. No more bailouts. Get it together already." Then the words I heard in my sleep for many nights thereafter: "Please, don't call 'til you're sober."

"I understand. And I'm going to make it all the way back, Luke. I promise."

"Good-bye."

I wasn't sure I knew exactly *where* he'd make it back, but I hoped it wasn't to Manhattan.

CHAPTER
4

It was hard not to think of 9/11.

The coverage, the networks' slick graphics and official storm logos. The death toll.

The pain.

Maybe I watched so much TV during the days following Katrina because I couldn't turn off my photographer's inner lens. It saw more than the water and filth, it saw the survivors' eyes crying for help. Many cried with their mouths too, cursing at camera crews and pleading for rescue.

Some also cried with cardboard signs:

WHERE'S FEMA?

PAGING BUSH & CHENEY!

LOOTERS WILL BE SHOT

KATRINA KILLED MY BABY

NAGIN LIED

During a commercial I sat back on the futon and relaxed my

neck and shoulders. I hadn't noticed how sore they'd become from my leaning forward and craning toward the TV hour after hour. That realization made my eyes hurt. And once again I was drawn back to the memories of September 11th and felt the toll the constant coverage had taken on my mind and soul.

I decided some fresh air and lunch in Little India would serve me well. As was my custom, I carried my camera along. The walk was energizing.

I was sitting in Pio Pio's in Jackson Heights when my cell phone rang and displayed an unfamiliar number from area code 504.

"Hello?" I answered.

The man's low smoker's voice was unfamiliar. "This Luke Millward?"

"It is."

"Jerome Harris callin' from New Awlins."

I switched my cell phone from one ear to another. "What can I do for you?"

"Your father is Charles?"

"Yes." I wondered if this call might come. I never imagined I'd be sitting in a Peruvian restaurant.

"Have you heard from 'im?"

"Not lately, no."

"How long it been?"

"Two years, maybe more."

Just then I remembered a larger-than-usual package I'd received a couple of months ago from Dad. I hadn't bothered to open it. It was the most recent in a string of packages that arrived every six months or so from some new zip code. They usually contained an odd trinket Dad had bought or occasionally one of his random personal belongings he wanted me to have. I'd always wondered if sending old car keys or a lucky dice keychain from Vegas was his way of making peace. When I asked, he'd said he just wanted me to have those things in case something ever happened to him.

Like all the others packages, it was stacked in a corner of my apartment building's storage closet.

"What's this about?" I asked the man.

"Your daddy is missin', Luke. Been livin' here in New Awlins for 'bout a year."

Here it comes, I thought, closing my eyes.

"Nobody's seen 'im since a couple Sundays ago. Night before—"

"Katrina."

"Tha's right. He's been teachin' and playin' with me and my guys at a place on Chartres Street for on about seven months. Livin' in a place in the five-four."

"Five-four?"

"Lower Ninth, son."

I imagined his body was one of those rotting in a public

restroom or floating facedown and bloated under a bridge somewhere.

So this is what it feels like to be an orphan. "I'm sorry to hear
that, sir." The words carried unexpected uneasiness. *My father is
dead.*

"Don't be sorry, Luke. Get on down here and find 'im."

"Excuse me?"

"It's why I'm callin'."

"Won't someone just call me when he's found?"

"You kiddin'? You must not got a TV."

Point taken.

"Even the good-meanin' guys down here don't have the time
for much of that." He paused. "Come find your father, Luke Millward. For alls we know he's alive somewhere. Most our cell phones
aren't workin'—he could be hurtin' somewhere, or in San Antonio or up north. We're hopin' he is. We're prayin' it."

"Even if I wanted to, I can't just pause my life and go on a
wild-goose chase. I just can't."

"Then do it for his fiancée."

"Come again?" I switched my cell phone back to the other ear.
"My father was engaged?"

"To a wonderful one. Gettin' married sometime 'fore Christmas."

Who is she? I thought.

"Luke, she's my kid sister." He let the words have impact. "Her name is Jez."

Jez. I didn't know what shocked my system more: my father's probable death or a woman marrying a practicing alcoholic who had a premonition problem.

"I'll call you back," I said. "This number on my caller ID, it's yours?"

"It's one of the club's cell phones. Call it anytime. But service is hit-and-miss, know that."

"I'll call back."

"Soon?"

"Yes, sir. Good-bye. And thanks." I hung up and stepped out of the restaurant and into the noise of the city. I moved through the crowded afternoon streets toward the subway.

I don't remember riding it home.

That night I sat in my apartment with Jordan and listened as she repeated back to me the details of Jerome's call. She seemed to hear things in the story I hadn't said.

"This guy, Jerome, he was your dad's best friend."

"Who knows?"

"And your dad is getting married to this guy's sister—or was anyway . . ." She scratched my back. "Sorry."

"No need."

"I have to wonder, how did he get your number? You should ask him that. What if this is some sort of scam? I see this a lot."

"Jordan, it's not a scam."

"Probably true, but still, how did he find you? You sure he doesn't want money or something? Maybe he thinks you're loaded because you helped your dad when he needed it."

I'd forgotten I'd ever told her that. "I haven't sent Dad money in a long time. Not since last time we spoke."

"Still, Luke, I'd ask. How'd he find you?"

I agreed it was a smart question and promised to pose it when I called Jerome back.

"Huh. Your dad was living in New Orleans." She looked down at her Diet Dr. Pepper. "You've hardly told me a thing about him."

Not much to tell. I haven't talked much about my mother either.

We picked at our sesame chicken and brown rice.

"So you're going," she asked. "Right?"

"I dunno yet."

"You've got to go, Luke. Just to know, for sure, you've got to."

"I dunno."

She took both my hands. "I'll go with you."

"You can't leave right now, Jordan. Not at the end of the quarter. You've got closings to push through."

"Yes I do, but I'd go with you if you asked."

We returned to our Chinese food while the Killers' *Hot Fuss* played on the living room stereo.

An hour later I hugged Jordan good-bye at the elevator in my building and got ready for bed. The bathroom mirror reminded me of the dark circles under my eyes that I'd inherited from my father. When I was particularly tired or stressed I looked like I'd been popped in both eyes. The rest of the time I looked like a raccoon. When I was young, Mom said they were so dark because I was an only child. If they'd had more children the effect would have spread across the other kids.

I cued up a classical playlist on my iPod. Tracks from the Boston Pops, some Mozart, newly added songs from a Jenny Oaks Baker CD that Jordan had given me for my birthday. I killed the lights, put in my headphones, and for a moment Jenny's majestic violin transformed my room into a concert hall, drowning out the steady stream of horns and sirens below.

My mind dropped sheets over the images of Katrina's wrath.

♩♩♩

Mom wasn't always unhappy.

Dad wasn't always a drunk.

Just before my sophomore year of high school—the year before Grandma died—the three of us took a road trip to Yankees spring training at Legends Field in Tampa Bay. Mom let me ride up front for most of the trip while she read or slept in the backseat of our white Saab. Dad drove us east through Shreveport, Jackson, Mobile, and across the Florida Panhandle. Each stop brought a little history from Dad's AAA guidebook, a keychain for Mom's collection, and snacks.

I bet Mom ate fifteen pounds of licorice on that trip. It's funny, I used to tease Mom about her addiction to those little bags of Nibs.

Dad's official travel treat was Tab cola and Planters salted peanuts. I remember him dropping a few peanuts at a time to the bottom of every can as Mom playfully teased, "You're gross. Yuck. Who puts peanuts in their soda?" Even *Dad* couldn't explain the appeal, but I don't recall a single mile of that trip, or any other for that matter, when Dad didn't have a can in his hand or at-the-ready in his cup holder. I always threatened to tell when Mom stole sips as Dad pumped the gas or checked the tires. But all she had to do was slip me a handful of licorice and I'd pledge to keep her secret for another leg of the trip. I didn't even like licorice.

My staples were Twinkies, Ho-Hos, and Big League Chew, the only bubblegum worthy of a little leaguer. That is, unless you were crazy Mrs. Armstrong's kid. She made a big show one day at practice that Big League Chew was a "gateway candy" to those fake cigarettes, then real cigarettes, then real snuff. So Mrs. Armstrong banned it from the dugout and told her son, Magic Mikey, our only left-handed pitcher, that she'd make him chew a hundred packs at once if she ever again caught him with the stuff. Dad said some things weren't worth fighting over.

Sometimes, when he and the other coach were working with

the infielders, I'd take a couple guys behind the dugout and give them a wad of the shredded pink gum from its tinfoil pouch. Few things are more exhilarating for a thirteen-year-old than providing forbidden bubblegum to a teammate. Not long after Mrs. Armstrong's ban took effect, Dad stopped at a Circle K on the way to practice and came out with three packs of Big League Chew. "Just in case." He winked. "You never know when you might run low."

My dad told me that Mrs. Armstrong was a sweet woman who just had a few "issues." I guess he thought I should know what that meant. I didn't. I was only a right fielder.

On that spring training vacation, Mom sat reading in the stands for hours while Dad and I jostled for autographs and fought professional sports memorabilia hounds and little kids alike for signatures and foul balls. She smiled so kindly when I arrived at our spot above the third base line with a ball I'd caught off a rookie's splintered bat. I can't even remember his name anymore.

"That's spectacular!" Mom took the ball from me and pretended to examine it. "I bet this will find a special spot in your room, won't it, dear?"

"Sure will!"

Dad bought us matching, old-school, cotton Yankee baseball caps. I misplaced mine a couple months later and never found it again.

I think that was the same year we met Billy Crystal in the

parking lot. Mom took our picture, and Mr. Crystal signed my pennant. I bet I held it on my lap for at least a hundred miles on the way to Atlanta.

I remember Dad talking Mom into taking an eight-hour detour to Georgia to visit a friend from college. This man arranged for a special VIP tour of Coca-Cola's headquarters. We got free hats, red-and-white T-shirts, and some Coke samples in little glass bottles that Mom kept calling "precious" and "cute." I'm sure Mom couldn't have cared less. Still, she plugged along.

"It might not have been my *favorite* thing to do," she said to Dad and me as we rolled out of town the next morning en route to our home in Texas. "But neither was seeing that mini-league baseball match. It doesn't matter though, because I love to see you two happy. If *you're* happy, *I'm* happy."

That wouldn't be true for long.

CHAPTER
5

I awoke and withstood the temptation.

It wasn't easy.

The television wanted to be on, and I wanted to hear how things had progressed overnight in New Orleans and the surrounding area. I wondered how many more victims had been found in attics or in submerged cars. Was my father among them?

How is Bernard holding up?

I showered, shaved, threw on my favorite pair of jeans and a New Jersey Nets sweatshirt, ate a bowl of Corn Pops, and grabbed my cell phone and camera. Then I set the cell phone back on the kitchen counter and walked out the door. Free from distractions. Free from expectations. Free from the man who wanted me to unplug my life and travel to his city in mourning.

Even four years after the attacks of September 11th, Ground Zero was still a powerful place to sit and absorb the ambiance. It was also a unique setting to capture human goodness on film.

Foot traffic increased each year during the days leading up to the anniversary, and the mood was reverent, respectful, resolute.

While others snapped away without regard for the historic setting, I *always* asked permission, *never* intruded when it was obvious someone needed privacy, and *always* felt guilty no matter how friendly or grateful the subject was.

I walked around and chatted with a few tourists. What brought them to New York? Where were they on 9/11? What did they think of Mayor Bloomberg's plans for the memorial?

I watched people process the giant hole in the ground for the first time. I watched a father take a photo of his daughter with a police officer on the viewing platform. It reminded me of the time Dad stopped an off-duty firefighter in a Dallas Sabarro's and insisted on paying for his lunch.

On previous trips I'd met some of the most fascinating people at the site that changed America forever. Survivors, neighbors, mothers and fathers of the fallen. I once met a young woman named Kellie whose childhood friend, Liz, had been killed that September morning. She carried in her purse one of the many letters Liz had written to her over the years. "I have every letter she ever sent me," Kellie told me. "They are a small piece of her." I admired Kellie's spirit.

On this day I met a husband and wife from India who had made Ground Zero their top priority during their first-ever visit to the States. They knew no one who'd died, knew no one who'd survived, knew absolutely no one in any way connected with the tragedy. But they respected freedom and grieved for the slain innocent.

I asked if I could take their photo; they posed with somber eyes and mouths. They wrote their names on my notepad so I could spell them correctly later when I tagged the photo. I asked to shoot one last picture of them from behind. They each shook my hand and walked on.

I captured them strolling slowly away, holding hands. The woman's head resting on her husband's shoulder, her hand tucked in her coat pocket. They disappeared.

I sat.

♩♩♩

Not everyone in our Fort Worth, Texas, suburb had grass, but we did. Mom wanted grass and Dad wanted Mom to be happy. So when he designed our home, Dad included a top-of-the-line sprinkler system. Even during the driest of droughts, Mom had her grass. It was thick, dark green grass that made your legs itchy if you sat in it too long. Grass that looked like it had been stolen from Augusta National Golf Club in Georgia.

Fortunately for all of us, Dad liked cutting the grass almost as much as Mom enjoyed watching it grow from her reading chair on the top of the three-tiered deck on the back of the house. Dad pulled the mower from his custom-built shed every Saturday morning before the sun rose to its peak and the air became so hot it could melt the blades of grass together. He sometimes mowed it like a baseball diamond, creating elaborate patterns that made Mom smile.

Mom would watch from her spot, reading a book or knitting or just sitting with her eyes closed and a glass of lemonade in her hand.

And then the phone would ring.

Every Saturday, Grandma Fleek would call at 10:00 AM to check in. Every single Saturday. The phone would ring, but neither Dad nor I would dare to answer it. Mom would pick it up and disappear somewhere in the house. The calls were so important to both Mom and Grandma that Mom wouldn't leave the house on Saturdays for errands until the call came and ended. Even if Mom had spoken to Grandma four times during the week, which often happened, Grandma still called on Saturday morning. Even if Mom had inadvertently hurt Grandma's famously sensitive feelings, which also often happened, the call still came. It was their "make good" time.

And it always worked.

I was washing the car in the driveway one Saturday in June of 1990 as Dad made a careful, final pass around some landscaping stones. The mower was too loud for either of us to hear the phone ring, but at some point we both noticed Mom talking on the cordless phone from her chair.

I looked at my Swatch. It was 9:17 AM.

She stood abruptly. A few seconds later, she dropped her book and her hand went to her mouth.

The scream that followed was so loud we could have heard it over a thousand mowers.

Then Mom dropped the phone and fell to her knees.

Dad and I raced to her side.

Mom's voice trembled. "My mother, my mother."

Dad picked up the phone and was introduced to Nikki Van De Car, an officer with the El Paso police department.

Grandma was dead.

"What?"

"A fatal car accident, sir."

"Accident? Where?"

"El Paso. Two miles from her home, sir. I'm so sorry to make this call, to have upset your wife."

"When?"

"Early this morning. Three cars. Appears to be a DUI. Mrs. Fleek and the driver of the second car both died at the scene. Witnesses say the third driver, a Mexican citizen, lost control while intoxicated and ran a red light downtown."

"You mean an illegal?"

"The investigation is ongoing, sir."

"Are you sure it's her? You're absolutely sure? She never drives alone, *never.*"

"There was a passenger, sir. Her neighbor, we believe. Mary Henry. She's stable at Thomason Hospital. It appears they'd been to breakfast about a block from the crash."

Dad opened the sliding glass door off the deck and stepped into the house. "You've arrested him, right? What's his name?" Anger began to wedge its way between Dad's words.

"We'll speak further when you arrive."

"But there *will* be an arrest? There will be charges?"

"Tend to your family, sir, and we'll speak again soon. Again, my condolences. Our department's condolences."

Dad returned outside and looked down at Mom. I sat by her on the floor of the deck, stroking her hair and letting my own tears fall and merge in rivers down both cheeks. Every few minutes Mom looked up and gasped for air and tried to ask Dad a question.

"We'll leave today," Dad said to the officer. "Where do we go?"

"The remains will be held at Thomason. We'll need you to formally identify—"

"Of course."

The officer gave Dad her contact information, repeated her condolences, and hung up.

Dad and I helped Mom into bed. He kissed her forehead and repeated, "I'm here, it's OK, I'm here. It's all going to be OK. Shhh."

Later Dad left us alone while he made the travel arrangements. I sat on the side of Mom's bed, just as she had sat on mine almost every night when I was a child.

I wanted to cry when Mom told me she'd bickered with Grandma on the phone that Tuesday. She'd accused Grandma of trying to guilt her into planning an extended visit to El Paso that summer.

"Maybe we won't come at all this year," Mom had snapped.

"Your choice. You know where I am," Grandma answered.

Those were the last words they spoke to one another.

Mom cried on and off all afternoon. She asked questions I didn't know the answers to. She asked questions no teenager should ever have to know the answers to.

The trip to bury Grandma next to Grandpa passed in a blur. The funeral was a short and simple one. Mary Henry was still recovering at the hospital, but her three children came to honor Grandma. A few friends from church and the seniors' center also came. Both of Grandma's sisters lived in Michigan and neither one was healthy enough to travel.

Of course Grandpa had been dead for years, and like Dad and me, Mom was an only child. There was no one else.

We were home and cutting the grass again before any of us had time to process the accident and consider life without Grandma, without the Christmas fudge, the hugs that smelled like vitamins, the phone calls to share her silly knock-knock jokes.

Mom didn't sleep well after the trip. She had nightmares and struggled with a toxic blend of depression at being orphaned and anger at the man who'd killed her mother with his truck and a dozen beers.

Dad finally suggested she see a doctor to get help sleeping. "The sooner we get you sleeping well, back in a routine, and comfortable, the sooner you can get back to school. The kids miss you, honey."

Dad also asked her to see a counselor who could help her learn to live with her new set of emotions. When therapy didn't work, they tried antidepressants. When the pills didn't work, they tried new pills. The doctor's kept writing prescriptions and Dad kept filling them until Mom could have slept through Desert Storm.

She was practically dead when she slept and only slightly more alert when she was awake. Meanwhile the school told Dad she could take as much time as she needed. Her friends suggested "more aggressive" treatment for the depression, having no idea that her dependence on the pills was becoming the greater concern. Dad didn't care how it happened. He just wanted to save her.

I just wanted my mother back.

CHAPTER

6

It had been three days since Jerome called.

"You can't ignore this, Luke." Jordan sat next to me in a booth in a deli on 7th Avenue.

I took a bite of my dill pickle.

"He might think you're coming, already on your way even. You can't leave him wondering, Luke. You can't."

I reminded myself she was helping, or at least trying to.

"I'm sorry. I know this is your thing. I just want to help." She began spreading a second layer of cream cheese on her onion bagel.

"I know you do." I finished my pickle. "I should call him back, at least to tell him I can't make it. That's the right thing to do."

"You're serious?"

"Of course."

"You're not going to go look for your father? You're not

interested? Curious? He could be alive somewhere. He could be looking for you."

"Jordy, he's got my cell. He'd call."

"Unless he's in trouble."

I shook my empty soda cup and reached across to grab hers.

"Luke, you're right, it's none of my business. I'm sorry I keep pushing."

I drank her soda until the straw pulled up the final noisy drops. "I just . . . I just don't know what I'd gain by going on an expedition. If he was in New Orleans when the storm hit, and if his friends haven't seen or heard from him, he's probably gone. And I'm OK with that. I know his heart was good, even though we'd drifted apart. There were no hard feelings between us the last time we spoke. No regrets." I said the words hoping they'd *feel* true. They didn't.

"Then I support you. Whatever is best for you. I'm all in."

♩♩♩

All in. I remember the first time I heard Dad say those words. Dad's friend Kaiser suggested a poker night during the holidays the year Grandma died. He showed up with five or six guys from the firm and a pack of brand-new cards from Caesars Palace he'd picked up on a business trip to Vegas. That first night they sat around a table in the basement drinking beer and playing Texas Hold'em. I was supposed to be glued to a movie on the huge rear-projection

TV dad had bought, but poker and its strategies fascinated me. Probably more than that, I just liked hearing Dad laugh.

That night became the first of many poker nights. It didn't take long at all for Dad to purchase a real poker table. He also bought a special table for the cashier, real poker chips, a silly dealer's visor, and an expensive safe to put the cash in.

He said it wasn't complete until he built the bar in the basement to go with it.

Sometimes I watched. Sometimes Dad had his guys play a round with pretzel sticks so I could sit in. Mom didn't seem to mind when I asked her what she thought about it. She didn't mind much of anything.

Dad's group played every Friday night. And though Dad didn't always win, they always played in *his* basement where he could keep an eye on Mom and be there if she needed him.

Dad was lonely during Mom's final year, but he was also resolute that she'd survive and break her addictions. He prayed for her as she shuffled in a slow circuit from her bed to the refrigerator to the couch in the living room to the medicine cabinet and back to bed. He prayed she would feel better, sleep better, be in a better mood when she woke from her daylong naps. He prayed her mood swings would ease.

He prayed he could save her.

Sadly, I don't think Mom ever grasped just how lonely Dad had become without her.

On rare occasions, Mom could be talked into dinner out or a Sunday drive, but I think she did it to appease us more than the chance to breathe fresh air or remind herself what Fort Worth looked like. We dragged her to a couple of Dallas Mavericks basketball games—which she didn't pretend to enjoy—and a movie or two.

And Dad kept asking, even though she stopped saying yes.

"I'll never stop asking, sweetheart, because I love you."

"I know, Charles, I know. But let me sleep now. I'm exhausted."

"How about a trip up north? Oklahoma City next week?"

"You've got to work, Charles."

"I could take a few more days."

"You've already taken weeks, Charles. Maybe next month. I'll go next month."

She didn't.

"Sweetheart, you up for breakfast out? Pancakes? Waffle House? Maybe we could stop by the nursery after and you could help me pick some new plants for around the fountain in the front."

"No thanks, Charles. You and Luke go. Bring me back something to eat."

"Next time, then," Dad always said.

"Sure. Next time. I promise I'll go next time."

She didn't.

Right after Grandma died, Dad arranged for an in-home therapist to visit a few times. Mom was kind, she listened, she nodded at all the appropriate points. But when the counselor suggested it was time for Mom to respect her mother by going back to work, she asked Dad for a "short breather" from the sessions.

"But you'll see her again, right? She's really good, sweetheart. One of the best in the Metroplex."

"Yes, Charles, she is. Just not for a while. Just a breather. I'm really doing better. Truly better."

"All right then. A few weeks and you'll see her again?"

"I will."

She didn't.

CHAPTER

7

Larry Gorton's feet were in their usual position atop his desk.

"Knock, knock," I said, pushing his door open.

"Mr. Millward!" His voice was low and authoritative. "You, my former star pupil, have been delinquent. Please enter and tell me why you haven't come to visit me in such a long time that this old man can barely match your name to your face."

"You're not an old man—"

"Don't interrupt."

"You were done!"

"My office, my classroom, my rules."

I put an index finger to both sides of my head and pulled the trigger.

"Don't do that, Mr. Millward. I haven't got my camera out."

I laughed—easy to do in Larry's world. "It's good to see you, too. But it hasn't been that long, sir."

"Long enough. Long enough, young man, long enough."

"How have you been? Am I keeping you from something?"

"Yes, you're keeping me from my work, and for that I'm indebted to you, Mr. Millward."

"You don't have to call me 'Mister' anymore; I'm out of school." I'd said that every single time I'd seen my old professor since graduation from NYU. It never mattered.

"Are you still a Mr. Millward, Luke?"

"Of course, but we're not in class. I'm not a student. We're *peers* now." I'd said that before, too.

"Your last name, Mr. Millward, *defines* you." He put his hands on the back of his head, interlocked his fingers, and stretched back in his chair. "Your last name tells society who you are and where you came from, both in the short term and in the greater sense of where your ancestors' ship originated."

I smiled and repeated each and every one of those familiar words in my mind as he spoke them.

"You're right, as usual, Mr. Gorton." Those words were equally familiar.

"Then we agree to play by proper societal conventions." He put his feet on the floor and dramatically swiveled around to a mini-refrigerator on the floor. "Let's drink." He pulled out two small bottles of water.

"Thanks," I said, as he tossed me one.

He opened his and guzzled half the water. "How's work?"

"Work is great. I'm getting a lot of freelance projects. Even saying no to some now. I just can't take every job anymore."

"Listen, you do that as *infrequently* as you can. You never know which picture could change—"

"The world. I know."

Larry returned his feet to their home on his desk. Noticing the Oreo-sized holes in the heels of his socks only reminded me how much I had missed the man. Confident, kind, and maybe more comfortable with his place in life than anyone I'd ever known.

I suppose he reminded me a bit of Jordan. Maybe that's why I enjoyed being around them both.

I'd been a fence-sitter on photography until I entered his classroom for the first time. The art had always interested me, but like so many other passions it seemed impractical to turn art into industry and a hobby into a living. Hauling a camera around the world shooting pictures sounded glamorous and rewarding. But I knew few achieved the highest levels of success. Most never won awards or saw their work on newsstands or on Drudge. Sadly, few of the dreamers could make the leap from child shutterbug taking pictures on a disposable 35-millimeter to standing in the back of the White House Rose Garden shooting images of the president and leader of the free world.

I wanted that back then, but my heart and head didn't believe I had the eye.

Thank goodness Larry Gorton thought I did.

"Mr. Millward, what can I do for you? You bring me pictures to gush over?"

"No, sir, not this time. Just visiting. Checking in."

He chugged the rest of his water and shot the bottle hard across his office, using the wall as a backboard, watching it bounce around the rim and settle in the trash can. His raised both arms above his head. "That's a three."

I grinned and fidgeted with Larry's plastic Rudy Giuliani bobblehead doll.

"What's on your mind, kid?"

"Sir?"

He lowered his eyes and folded his arms across his sweater-vest.

"I don't know, I guess I just wanted to say hi. I'll let you get back to work." I returned Rudy to his spot on Larry's desk and stood.

"Sit."

I obliged.

"You're a horrible poker player, Luke Millward."

You have no idea.

"How's your father?"

It was my turn to chug the rest of my water bottle. I tossed it toward the trash can. Missed. "Figures."

"You heard from him lately?"

"Not exactly." As my academic mentor, Larry had known bits

and pieces of my personal history. He knew Mom was dead from prescription drug abuse, and he had met Dad once during my freshman year at NYU. But sitting there I couldn't recall how much I'd told him about Dad.

"You hear from him much anymore?"

"It's been a while, sir."

"How long?"

"A couple years, I guess, maybe a little less." I picked up the bobblehead doll again.

"He still drinking?"

I nodded.

Larry did, too. "That's a shame. . . . Tough life you've lived, young man. I bet your mom would be proud."

I nodded once more.

"Then tell me, Mr. Millward, what else is going on in your exciting, jet-setting life? Is there a woman?"

"Not really. Dates here and there. I'm hanging out a lot with a girl I met in school—Jordan Knapp."

"Good woman?"

"Sure is. We're just friends though. No time for a relationship right now."

"Does *she* know that?" he asked.

"That we're just friends?"

He nodded.

"Sure she does."

Wait for it.

"Good. And let's not forget the most important relationship, the one with our lens, you remember?"

I laughed despite myself. "Of course." I mocked his deep voice. "'The eternally intimate relationship between life and lens.' How could I forget?"

Larry smiled and probably congratulated himself on another job well done. Few professors took as much pride in the finished product than Larry Gorton did.

The two of us sat and enjoyed the rare silence that comes when two people trust one another. Eventually the chatter resumed. Politics, Iraq, the rash of paparazzi incidents in LA, Katrina, Rudy's rumored run for the White House in 2008, the Yankees. He showed me photos he'd taken earlier that summer on a trip to China. The pictures were captivating enough to take my mind off Jerome Harris. Almost.

"Can I ask you for some advice?" I finally said.

"Of course, that's why you came." He checked his clock. "I've still got time. Class starts in twenty-five."

"I got a call the other day from a man in New Orleans."

"After Katrina?"

"Yes."

"Proceed."

"This man, Jerome—a native I'm guessing—he called to tell me he knew my father. He'd been living in New Orleans."

Larry put his feet back on the floor and leaned onto his desk. There was never a better listener.

"He said he played with my father in a band. They both live in the Lower Ninth Ward."

Larry's eyes asked for more.

"My father is missing. No one has seen him since last Sunday."

"Before landfall."

"Yes, sir. And now they're all worried. Worried he's dead somewhere, or worse—injured, in trouble, something . . ."

"And this Jerome, you've never met him?"

"No."

"Any reason to doubt him? To mistrust?"

"Don't see why."

Larry studied my face. His eyes processed the scene. "You think your father is dead."

I stood and walked to the trash can, picking up the bottle that had landed on the floor and dropping it in.

"Hmm." Larry leaned back in his chair again, rubbing his face before lacing his hands behind his head.

"Would *you* go?" I asked.

"I don't do hypotheticals, you ought to remember that. Trust your eyes and the lens, nothing else."

That was precisely what I knew he'd say from the second I

pushed open his office door. I examined a line of photos in matching black frames on his back wall.

"You could always take your camera," Larry said.

"Sir?"

"Take your camera to New Orleans. Make the drive. The airport is probably still closed anyway."

"Drive from New York to New Orleans."

"Uh-huh."

"That's a long way, an *awfully* long way."

"They do make maps, Mr. Millward. There is even this crazy
new thing called the interweb—all the kids on campus are talking
about it. Some of these interweb places even give turn-by-turn
directions. Imagine that."

I looked for something to throw.

"I'm serious about this, young man. Make the trip. Take your
camera. Blog it. Stop at other cities along the way. New Orleans
isn't the only area cleaning up."

I took a deep breath and exhaled loudly. I ran my fingers
through my hair. My stomach flittered. I looked at my watch and
put on my jacket.

"Mr. Millward, you've seen a lot of suffering in your life;
you've seen parts of the world most of my students will only see
in the fantastic pictures you've taken. But you've never seen what's
happening in the Gulf. You've never seen this kind of human
event. Go. Capture it. Educate us. Honor them."

I knew you'd be good, I thought. *I didn't think you'd be* that good.

"OK, then, I'll let you get to class. Thank you." We shook hands.

"You'll go?"

"We'll see." I said good-bye and put my hand on the doorknob.

"Luke."

I turned to face him.

"Go recover your father."

CHAPTER

8

Larry Gorton was right.

Unfortunately, having correctly predicted what he would say didn't make hearing it any easier.

I needed to make the trip. Find closure. Photograph the scenes. Give the man a proper burial back in Texas. All true. Part of me felt relieved that at least death would have ended his temporal addictions, freed him from his greatest flaws, and released him from the loneliness he'd wrapped himself in since Mom's death.

I reminded myself again that he hadn't always been the man I'd spoken to on the phone two years ago. Anxious. Desperate. Running. Addicted.

Alone.

I also reminded myself that he hadn't been the one driving the truck that killed my grandmother. He hadn't been the lazy doctor who so willingly prescribed pills to my mother that she didn't need. And he hadn't been the one who abused those pills and buried his head in the sand of depression.

Dad hadn't been the one who refused to notice the sun was still rising, even though she wasn't.

Even though we've grown apart, I still want the best for him.

It felt good to think that.

I hadn't allowed myself to consider any alternatives. I was sure Dad had been killed in the storm or its aftermath and his body was waiting somewhere to be identified and claimed.

But what if he *hadn't* been killed? What if my father was unreachable in Houston or Baton Rouge or some other far-flung city? What if he'd boarded a bus and chosen to start over wherever it dumped him off? What if he wanted this? What if he wanted me to find him and forgive him and write a song with him?

I pushed that awkward notion aside long enough to call Jordan and ask her to meet me at six o'clock for an early dinner at our favorite Thai restaurant a few blocks from my building.

She walked in, on time as always, and glided into the chair across from me.

"This seat taken?"

"I'm going."

She smiled and took my hands in hers.

"Alone? You're sure?"

I smiled. "Yes."

♩♩♩

My mother and father were native Texans and high school sweethearts. Dad had been "going with" Mom's biology lab partner, Becky Ravenscroft, and every day they ate lunch together on hard round orange stools attached to the last rectangular table at the back of the cafeteria.

On an otherwise uneventful Thursday afternoon, Dad was eating a Fluffernutter sandwich on Wonder Bread and chatting with Becky when he saw my mother glide in the back door of the cafeteria. She was carrying nothing but a brown paper bag.

Dad had never seen this girl before. "She moved in slow motion," he described. "Her hair was so well-coifed. Her blush so immaculately applied. Her teeth so pearly white."

Dad said she parted the crowd like the Red Sea and walked toward him, scanning left and right for a seat. Just as she saw Dad, the school's all-state tight end yelled and waved at Becky from three tables away. "Becky Ravenscroft! You good at geometry?"

Becky hopped up and scampered to the "athlete's table."

Mom, oblivious, saw only a lonely young man sitting at the last table in the cafeteria. She approached the boy she would one day marry. "Mind if I sit here?"

"Sure," Dad said.

"You mind?"

"No! I mean *no* I don't mind. Sure you can sit here." Dad's palms were so sweaty he had to set his sandwich down and wipe his hands on his jeans under the table.

She sat down and began pulling her lunch out one item at a time—plastic bag with Fritos, plastic bag with four pieces of celery, plastic bag with a Fluffernutter sandwich.

Dad said he knew right then he'd spend the rest of his life stocking their pantry with marshmallow cream and peanut butter. Within a week, Dad finally had the great new girlfriend he deserved, and Becky had to find a new lab partner. The new couple was inseparable for the remainder of their junior year and right through high school graduation.

They stayed together, even when Dad was ready to sprint past first base but Mom wanted to save herself for marriage because she'd promised her mother on her sweet sixteenth that she would. Dad *strongly* suggested she wear more modest clothes. Mom suggested he take cold showers.

When Mom wanted to go to SMU instead of Texas A&M, Dad changed his plans and followed her.

When Dad had a dream during his freshman year that one day he'd design buildings on earth and a temple in heaven, Mom encouraged him to quit premed and study architecture.

Not a year later, Mom decided her heart wanted to teach elementary school children instead of pursue a doctorate and become a professor. Dad bought her a Snoopy thermos and filled it with daisies.

Then Dad felt inspired to spend a semester abroad studying architecture in Italy. Mom took a semester off and followed him.

So when Dad got down on one knee in the shadow of the Leaning Tower of Pisa and asked if she'd make his dreams come true, the answer was easy.

"Yes."

CHAPTER
9

The bags waited for me by the door.

Still, I wasn't convinced I was going. I'd packed the carry-on-sized suitcase I'd used to travel the world. My laptop and camera bags were ready to go. And over the last twenty-four hours I'd successfully cleared my schedule for a week.

Clients were appeased. Kirky, my agent, was supportive, probably because he wanted to see the shots. Of course Jordan thought I was already on my way out the door and made me promise to call from the road at the end of my first day. She hid it well, but I knew she wasn't thrilled I'd chosen to handle the burden alone. I'd made the case that she had her good name and a lot of money riding on several high-profile closings. She should stay.

Frankly, the truth was a pretty good reason, too. Her joining me would have felt very serious. Very adult. Very much like something a couple would do.

Since sitting down with Larry I'd avoided watching the news

or going beyond ESPN.com on the Internet. This freed my consciousness to make a rational choice, not one mired in the emotionally-draining images still floating north from the Gulf region. Once the television was on, I knew how challenging it would be to turn it off.

My wallet was in my front pocket. The lights were off. I'd locked a few valuables in a safe hidden in a cabinet under my bathroom sink. The Sebring I'd rented online was waiting for me on a Hertz lot in Greenwich Village.

It took three tries but I finally reached Jerome. "I'm coming."

"Good. I was startin' to wonder 'bout you."

"Yes, sir. Any news on my father?"

"Not yet, but lots of friends lookin', keepin' eyes open, and askin' 'round. And 'member now, other folks missin' too. Lots of 'em."

"Understood."

"Get comin' then. You got the number?"

"It's in my cell." I suddenly remembered Jordan's curiosity. "May I ask how you found me? My number?"

"Your dad gave it to Jez, in case anythin' ever happened."

"Of course."

"All right then. Come by the club Verses, on Chartres. Almost at the corner of Toulouse in the Quarter. We're 'bout the only thing here. But don't expect no music playin' right now. Just gatherin' up and seein', makin' sure we know who's survived here. Get comin', son."

"I will."

"And bring a photo."

"I will."

We thanked each other and hung up. I took my laptop back out of its bag, powered it up, and plugged it into my photo printer on my desk. I printed the most recent photo I could find of my father. We were standing side by side on the street outside my first NYU apartment. I repacked my laptop.

The other bags still waited for me by the door.

There were 1,306 miles and two long days—maybe three if I wore out early—between New Orleans and me.

I looked at my watch. Nearly noon.

What's the point now?

I slid the bags aside with my foot, stepped out, and locked the door. Not five minutes later I was on the subway bound for Times Square and a ticket to whatever movie started next.

"Can I help you?" the young man behind the counter mumbled. He had the look of an hourly employee who resented selling a movie ticket in the middle of a weekday to a grown man who should have been at work.

I smiled and fought to assume the best about him. A useful nugget from my father. "Let's see, what's starting now?"

"Read the screen, man. There's *Junebug* in about twenty

minutes, *Dukes of Hazzard* at the same time, *Deuce Bigalow 2* after that, *Red Eye*—"

"That one any good?" I spotted his name tag. "Tracy?"

"It's cool, I guess. Got that girl Rachel McAdams in it. She's hot."

I gave him two thumbs up and a goofy grin from my side of the glass.

"You get to see a lot of movies, huh? Nice gig you got."

Tracy's face finally brightened slightly and he gave me the "You know it, dude," wink and smile. He looked back down at his screen again. "Then there's *Brothers Grimm*. Matt Damon's in it."

I'd seen it already, but still asked, "How about that? Decent? I'm sure you've seen it, yeah?"

"Nah, ain't seen it. Looks dumb."

"No doubt." I studied the board again.

"Or, if you don't much care 'bout missing a couple minutes, you could catch *A Sound of Thunder*. Ed Burns and that English dude, Kingsley. Some of the guys saw it last night, said it was pretty sweet."

"Hmm, never heard of it."

"This special travel agency takes these dudes back in time."

"Time travel? You sold me."

I paid Tracy for the ticket. He told me to have a good day, and I think he actually meant it. Inside the red ropes I spent twenty-two dollars on popcorn with enough butter—though it shouldn't legally be called that—to drown my arteries, an enormous box that held maybe eight or nine Milk Duds, and a large ice with Mr. Pibb sprinkled on top.

The theater was almost empty.

♩ ♩ ♩

The A-wing hallway was packed with hyper high school students. Teachers barked and prodded teens from one class to another. I had stopped at my locker just outside Mr. Balfe's AP business class when I heard Dad's voice coming from the direction of the front lobby.

"Luke!"

He was fast-walking down the hallway toward me.

"Dad? What are you doing here? Everything OK?" Mom had been gone only a couple months and my counselor at school said Dad was still grieving. I guess we both were.

He pushed past students in the crowded, narrow stretch of hallway and got close enough that I recognized his favorite sports bar on his breath.

"Everything's just fine. You want to break out of here?"

"What?" I looked around me. "Dad, I can't, I've got Balfe's class. Are you OK?"

"I'm great. Just bored. Took off early from work. Come see *What About Bob* with me downtown."

I looked Dad over. He was wearing sweat pants, a golf polo, and tennis shoes without socks.

"A movie? I can't, Dad."

He reached over and slammed my locker. His voice rose. "Come on, kiddo. Quit being so serious. Your grades are great. Everyone knows what we've been dealing with, right? Come on, let's go have some fun together."

"Dad, I've got a quiz today. I really can't."

A few of my friends at nearby lockers were tuned in.

"Fine." He looked broken. "See you at home." He turned around and began walking away.

"Wait, Dad." I grabbed his sleeve. "Maybe you should sign me out and I'll drive you home." I stepped closer. "You can sleep this off—"

"Hey, there's *nothing* to sleep off. I'm good."

"Right. I'm sorry." I noticed Mr. Balfe rounding the corner toward us. "Let's go."

"Yes, yes, yes. Let's see a matinee and make a memory."

"You're doing a pretty good job of that already," I whispered. I wasn't sure which of us should be more embarrassed.

As inconspicuously as possible, I pulled him alongside me and up the hall toward the office. I walked right past it and out the door.

"Yes! Here we come, Bill Murray!"

The Saab was parked in the fire lane. Dad handed me the

keys, and I opened the passenger side door. I tossed my book bag in the backseat and got in the driver's side. I hadn't quite mastered the stick shift, and as I lurched and screeched out of the parking lot, I looked in the rearview mirror and saw a gaggle of kids watching from the terrace by the flagpole.

Some of them laughed.

Some of them knew.

I don't recall much about the movie itself. I do remember buying Dad peanuts and a soda and sitting where we always did no matter the theater: eight rows back, middle section. Dad liked to sit right next to me; I preferred a seat in between so we could spread out. That day I remember giving in and sharing the armrest with him.

I also remember Dad crying.

CHAPTER

10

Traffic.

This is why I don't own a car.

I reminded myself of this fact several times as I navigated toward the Holland Tunnel and out of the city. I hadn't had to drive anywhere in over a year and hadn't even owned a car since high school. At 6:30 AM the city was already filling with cars and color-blind pedestrians.

The buildings became smaller and the highway exits farther apart as I headed west on 78 into Pennsylvania. Not feeling suffocated by skyscrapers was refreshing, but by my first fill-up, I missed the energy of the city. For all its flaws, and there are many, New York is a photographer's dream.

Interstate 78 led me to 81 and I began to drive south through Maryland, West Virginia, and into the lush Shenandoah Valley of Virginia. The leaves were only threatening to begin their dance into fall colors, and I almost wished I could park on the side of the road until they did. Instead I stopped for gas and gum in Strasburg and followed directions on a billboard to someplace called Crystal Caverns. I knew I didn't have time to take the tour.

I did anyway.

The caverns were fantastic and I made a mental note to tell Jordan about them when we spoke that night and to e-mail her the photos. It was the kind of thing the Brooklyn-bred girl would have appreciated.

When I returned to my car, armed with several dozen photos and more information about crystalline rimstone and calcite crystals than I could possibly ever use, I saw I'd missed two calls from the cell phone number Jerome had given me. I called back. No answer and a full voice mail box.

I drove on. Interstate 81 carried me south and gradually southwest through Woodstock, Harrisonburg, and Roanoke. By the time the odometer read five hundred miles, I'd been on the road nearly twelve hours. I pulled off in Blacksburg, Virginia, and, remembering that my credit cards would be useless in New Orleans, I stopped at an ATM and withdrew the max. Then I checked into a Best Western across the street.

I tapped into the hotel's Wi-Fi, downloaded my pictures, e-mailed a few to Jordan, and called to let her know I'd survived so far. I apologized for not calling the night before and promised to keep her updated.

I fell asleep listening to Norah Jones on my iPod.

I dreamt that night that I was in a grassy field with friends. A young woman appeared over a ridge wearing a white spring dress, twirling a pink parasol, and singing a song I'd never heard before. She practically glided down the hill toward me.

♩ ♩ ♩

Dad had his most important dream not long after he met Mom in high school.

He didn't tell her about it until well after they were married, and I didn't hear about it until Mom was already addicted to prescription drugs and mourning Grandma.

Dad and I sat across from one another at a Cracker Barrel.

"How's school?"

"OK, I guess."

"Just OK?"

"It's hard. All my teachers are treating me weird, even some of my friends."

"Because of Mom?"

"I guess."

Dad took a bite of pot roast. "It won't last. Mom will get through this."

"Soon?"

"I sure think so, son."

Our waitress dropped off a second basket of bread.

"It's hard, Dad, to see her just lying around all the time. Watching TV. Sleeping. Watching more TV."

"She's suffering, son, that's what people do sometimes when they're grieving."

I concentrated for a moment on buttering my third roll. Dad flagged down the waitress and asked for a refill of his Pepsi.

"You know Courtney?" I asked Dad.

"Harding? From the track team?"

"Yeah. Her dad died of cancer last year."

"That's right, I'd heard about that. How is she doing?"

"Really good." I added more butter to the second half of my roll. "She says her mom is doing good, too. She got a job at the Red Cross. Still sad, I'm sure, but pretty happy. Considering."

"Luke, I doubt they're happy."

"You know what I mean, Dad. Not *happy,* but dealing, you know? They're dealing with it all. Moving on as best they can."

I could tell Dad was weighing his words. Whenever he took extra time to calculate what to say next, or how much he thought he should say, he'd rub his right earlobe.

"I get it," he finally said. "But we have to be careful, son. Everyone grieves differently. Some people bounce right back. Some deal with the grieving process by working through it, staying busy, occupying their mind with other things. Other people, like your mother, need time alone. They need to move at their own speed. Rushing them, rushing *her,* would be a mistake."

I poked at the ice in the bottom of my cup with the straw. "She'll surface again, Luke."

The waitress must have thought I was hinting because she grabbed my glass and disappeared. Dad picked at his fried apples.

"What if she doesn't?" I asked him.

He slid his plate aside, wiped up the area around him with a napkin, and put his elbows on the table. "She will."

Dad then shared with me "the dream" he'd carried as a lifeline since high school. It wasn't his only dream, but it was the one that gave him hope when he needed it most.

It was two nights before Senior Prom, and Dad dreamt he stood on a long, straight country road lined with magnolia trees. He turned around and saw that the road began not far behind him. But in front of him, the road stretched as far and straight as he'd ever seen. "It was like God had drawn a straight line through the forest," Dad said.

At various points ahead, on both the left and the right, tree branches hung like thick, muscular arms over the road. Curious, Dad began to walk. Every now and then, without warning, the surface changed. From smooth, fresh pavement to loose gravel to red dirt, back to pavement, and then to uneven cobblestone.

The more he walked the more he noticed danger all around him. Animals crouched in the brush and behind trees. Narrowed white eyes followed him, darting from hiding place to hiding place. He didn't know their breed; he only knew to fear them.

He walked on.

A noise startled him from behind. Dad turned and the branches behind him suddenly swayed and swatted violently at the ground below. He quickly looked forward again but now, some thirty yards ahead, stood a woman. She wore a long, flowing white dress and faced away from him.

"It was your mother," Dad told me.

The woman began to walk away from him.

"Stop!" Dad yelled.

She walked on.

Dad also walked, faster now, and with each step he took, she took one of her own. The winds behind them grew stronger and played notes to the most frightening song Dad had ever heard.

Tender whimpers from ahead.

Dad couldn't be sure, but after all these years, after replaying the dream hundreds of times in his mind, Dad was convinced the woman was crying out for him.

"Are you OK?" Dad called out to her, but as soon as the words left his mouth they were carried away by a violent rush of air. It came from behind and filled every inch of the road, lifting the two of them off their feet and tossing them from one side of the road to the other.

The woman yelled to my father. "I . . . I can't . . . can't . . . breathe . . ." She was drowning in the energy of the air swooshing by them.

"Save me, Charles," the woman begged.

He reached out to her, and she locked her soft fingers and

palms around his wrists. The angry wind jerked and jostled them down the road. She continued to choke and sputter and her face turned a painful blue. But they were together now, joined tightly at both wrists.

Dad begged her to be strong, to breathe, to remain calm.

The woman cried tears that flew away in the air instead of hitting her cheeks.

Finally realizing he was the only one who could save her, Dad pulled her close with all his strength and filled his lungs with air.

Then he put his mouth to hers.

He breathed out slowly, emptying his chest.

Her eyes closed as she took his breath.

Once again, he took all the air he could and gently put his lips around her mouth and exhaled.

She opened her eyes and smiled. Just then Dad saw a large branch hanging out into the road. The woman let go of Dad's wrist with one hand and grabbed the branch as they passed by.

The wind clawed at their legs and the woman held on to Dad as long as she could. But when Dad sensed he was pulling her free from the safety of the sturdy branch, he said good-bye and let go.

Dad was swept down the road and out of sight.

The waitress dropped our check on the table and thanked us for coming.

Dad straightened up and looked me in the eye. "I don't know how," he said, "but I'm going to save your mother."

CHAPTER

11

The hotel's obnoxious wake-up call shook me to reality.

I've never understood why, but 6:00 AM comes earlier in hotel rooms than at home. I wiped my eyes and stretched out across my surprisingly comfortable king-sized bed. Thankfully the television remote was within reach.

I turned it on.

The coverage was still pervasive, but just as during 9/11 and other historically significant events of my lifetime, the broadcast and cable networks found a way to systematically begin sprinkling in other stories and reporting on lighter fare. Still, I thought the reporters looked embarrassed to be reporting results from dog shows and hot dog-eating championships.

The evacuation of the Superdome had been completed.

The 17th Street canal breach had been repaired and water was being pumped out of the city at last. Experts predicted dry streets by mid-October.

Rescue workers said there were a surprising number of hold-outs still refusing to leave the city behind.

Could Dad be one of those?

Bodies were still being identified and recovered on overpasses, left by broken and heartbroken family members before they boarded buses for new lives, whether they wanted them or not. In attics and in slowly emerging cars even more bodies were being discovered.

He's probably one of those.

The smell, one reporter says, is something you cannot describe. It's death and grief and filth typical of war, not an iconic American city. The woman, trying her best to hold it in, cuts the segment short. There's no point seeing her vomit on camera.

Highlights roll of a panel of talking heads from an overnight show. They debate whether Michael Brown should resign entirely from FEMA. They angrily mock his experience as a judge for the Arabian Horse Association.

Well, that can't possibly be true, I thought.

Later, the same panel discussed the outrage from House Minority Leader Nancy Pelosi and Senate Minority Leader Harry Reid. The two accused the president of mismanaging the disaster fallout and of a failure of leadership. Analysis turned to argument.

I muted the television.

My laptop was tucked under the bed. I pulled it up and used

my stomach as a desk. An extra pillow behind my head got me to the perfect height.

There was an e-mail from Mrs. Paisley, my perpetually concerned neighbor who hadn't seen me much lately and was worried I wasn't eating enough. There was a surprise note from Dan, a former roommate who was serving his last tour in Iraq and was beginning to worry about money and returning home to resume civilian life. He wondered if I'd let him stay with me for a bit while he got things in order.

There was also a short note from Larry wishing me luck on my trip and asking me to drop him a note or stop by campus when I returned to the city. I replied and thanked him for his concern.

My junk filter had also filled up nicely overnight with bulk e-mails from eBay, a political web site I'd never heard of, and from experts promising to enhance everything imaginable. One e-mail caught my eye. It was a touching, painful note from a gentleman named Dr. Clement Okon. He revealed that his uncle had been killed in a recent military coup in Nigeria and Dr. Okon had inherited ten million dollars. Sadly, he had no easy way to get it out of the country and away from the corrupt, greedy regime in power. Would I help him for a promise of two million dollars?

I smiled and forwarded it with an "LOL" to my buddy Dan in Iraq. "Your money woes are solved!" I added.

Before packing up and heading out I felt compelled to e-mail

Jordan and share Dad's dream. She was always accusing me—in her playful way—of not opening up as much as she did. She was right; she deserved more of me than I'd given, and having a written record while it was fresh in my mind seemed the appropriate thing to do. After all, it was unlikely Dad would ever tell that story again in the first person.

I concluded my note:

There you have it. It's fair to say that in her last days my mother was dismissive of the dream. Something about Dad thinking he was meant to save her made her even more bitter.

I remember Mom asking, "Why couldn't you have saved MY mother?" (Haven't told you much about my grandma. Someday I will.)

I also remember Mom saying, "It was a DREAM, Charles, a DREAM." Mom said that a lot. Dad always answered her saying it was "a premonition." Even when he corrected her, Dad was kind.

Come to think of it, I don't think Dad was ever anything BUT kind to my mother.

Dad said that he and Mom had this debate many times over the years, about what Dad's vivid dream might have meant. She used to think it was sort of romantic, I guess. Dad saving the day. A white knight. A hero in his dreams. The hero of her dreams. But as Mom slipped from reality and neared the veil, I guess she'd sort of minimized his dream to some kind of silly and childish quirk.

To Dad, though, his premonitions were an important part of who he was and what he'd accomplished. They mattered to Dad. THEY MATTERED.

Some were silly. For example, Dad always drove with trash bags, scissors, a funnel, a shovel, and duct tape in the trunk of his car. He said you never knew when you might need them. But we teased him relentlessly that he could never open the trunk in front of anyone for fear they'd think they were about to become a victim of some grisly crime. Dad said if I wasn't careful, I might be.

Other premonitions were serious. Like saving a life.

One last thing. I remember Dad didn't speak to me as we drove home from Cracker Barrel that evening in the winter of '90. (Early December, I think.)

But when he pulled the car into the garage and turned off the engine, we both unbuckled and he grabbed me in a hug. All the way home I'd been trying so hard not to cry. I remember the stick shift digging into my side.

Dad said, "Luke, I'm going to save your mother."

I hadn't felt so good since Grandma died. I cried like a baby.

There you have it. Thanks for listening. I don't deserve friends like you. ☺ I'll call tonight.

Luke

CHAPTER
12

By lunchtime I was in Knoxville, Tennessee.

I pulled into a McDonald's and sat in a corner booth with my Two Cheeseburger Meal and a cold Barq's. I unfolded the *USA Today* I'd picked up that morning in the lobby of the hotel. The Katrina images on the front page were captivating. The kind of pictures a photographer wishes he'd taken himself. I wondered how often someone saw one of my shots and wished they'd been the one holding the camera.

When I was young, Dad liked to drive by buildings and say, "See that one? Now *that's* an engineering marvel. I sure wish *I'd* designed it." He'd even been known to walk into some of the most eye-catching buildings and ask if he could give himself a tour.

Once, when I was assigned to write a paper in the ninth grade about a famous Texas landmark, Dad helped me narrow down the teacher's list of twenty or thirty choices. When I told Dad I thought the description for the Spanish Governor's Palace sounded pretty cool, he asked me if I'd like to see it in person.

"It's in San Antonio, Dad."

"So?"

"We live in Dallas."

"Your point is?"

I couldn't have talked Dad out of it even if I'd *wanted* to.

Two days later, on a Saturday, Dad woke me up at 6:00 AM and we drove three hundred miles south to San Antonio. Dad bought me a disposable camera on the way and two more from a gift shop. We visited the Spanish Governor's Palace and Dad walked through it with childlike wonder. We took a cruise down the two-and-a-half mile Riverwalk and bought Mom a keychain for her collection.

Then we ate at McDonald's. In fact, we ate at McDonald's four times that weekend.

I slid the newspaper aside and dialed Jordan's cell.

"Hey, I recognize that number," she said, answering the phone.

Her voice made me smile.

"What's up today?" I asked. Of course I wasn't terribly interested in what her schedule looked like, but the car had already become a lonely place and I wasn't even close to New Orleans.

"Same stuff," she said. "Hold on a minute."

I heard her office door creak shut.

"I got your e-mail."

"Good. Sorry if I rambled."

"Luke. Uh, hello? Don't be crazy. I loved it. That was quite a dream. And quite a guy, huh?"

"Quite a guy," I repeated, squeezing more ketchup onto a corner of my cheeseburger wrapper.

"So where are you?"

"Knoxville. Lunchtime."

She didn't have to ask. "Golden Arches."

"What can I say." I stuck five fries in my mouth and added what I always said when we had the "diet discussion." "I've got a thing for clowns."

"You know I'm rolling my eyes, right?"

"Why do you think I called?"

She laughed, I smiled, and for the first time that day I thought of something besides my father.

"Any news from the guy?"

"Jerome. And none. He called yesterday but I've not been able to get him on the phone. The news has been saying cell service in the city is pretty spotty. So who knows."

I heard the creaky door again.

"I hate to say it, but I've got to run."

"Hot lunch date?"

"I wish. No, I'm showing a place at 1:30."

"Of course. I gotta go, too. Lots of road still today."

"Drive safely?"

"Always."

"Call me tonight?"

"Sure."

"Luke?"

"Yeah?"

"You're the best."

"You, too."

♩ ♩ ♩

Dad believed in love at first sight.

He'd fallen for Mom instantly because one of his premonitions told him he would. And though he never pushed the same expectation on me, I always suspected he thought I'd meet my true love the same way.

Dad was in his den playing Eagles' songs on his guitar when I came home from my first official double date. Mom had probably been asleep for hours.

"So?" Dad asked.

"So what?"

"So how was it?"

"Awesome. *Really* awesome."

"*Really* awesome?"

I started giggling. "Yeah, Dad, thanks for letting me go. It was *really* fun."

"How fun?" Dad raised his eyebrows so high they looked like they'd been surgically replanted. "Hmm?"

"Come on, Dad, cut it out, it was fun. We had a fun time."

"So give me your O.G.T."

For as long as I've been alive, or at least as far back as I remember, my parents and I had a system for coaxing One Good Thing from each other about our days. Mom and Dad said there was always One Good Thing about even the very worst of days. At the dinner table, in the car, during a commercial on TV, it didn't matter—anyone could call for an O.G.T.

"Quit stalling over there and give me your O.G.T."

"Do I have to?"

Dad flicked his guitar pick at my head.

"Fine. My One Good Thing for today . . . This could be tough, what with all the *firsts* that happened tonight."

Dad's eyebrows shot up again.

"Gotcha!"

"Get on with it, before *my* O.G.T. involves you and an ambulance."

I took a seat on Dad's leather recliner and popped the leg rest up. "She let me hold her hand during the movie."

"Let you?"

"We kept bumping them in the popcorn bucket, so finally I just grabbed it and held it there."

"In the popcorn bucket?"

"Yeah."

Dad pretended to beat his head with the neck of his guitar.

I giggled some more.

"So you liked her."

"No, Dad, I didn't like her. She smelled like fish tacos and kept talking about Dungeons and Dragons all night. Booooring."

Now Dad was laughing, too.

"Of course I like her, old man. That's why I asked her out. She's awesome."

"And?"

"And nothing. Good time. Good movie. Awesome girl. Plus Jaime and Zac had a good time, too. We're totally doing it again."

"But she's not the one."

"The one?"

"The one you'll love."

"How am supposed to know *that?* I'm just a kid."

"You'd know. There's a spark when you're together that you can almost see. And there's a pain you can hardly bear when you're not. It's called being . . . *together.*"

"I guess I don't get it."

"You will. Trust me."

I spent the rest of the evening helping Dad write a song.

CHAPTER
13

I was only a hundred and ten miles from New Orleans.

But pushing on any farther wasn't an option. By 9:00 PM my eyes were bleary and my rear end was numb. Not to mention my growing concern at navigating through a darkened New Orleans still mostly underwater.

I pulled into a Holiday Inn Express in Hattiesburg, Mississippi. One corner of the parking lot was filled two-stories high with broken trees, small brush, and building debris.

"Hi. Can I get a room for the night?" I slid my license and credit card across the counter.

The woman greeting me in jeans and a T-shirt laughed. "Oh, sure."

"You're booked?"

"Um, yeah."

"I'll take whatever. Two double-beds. Maybe a suite? Anything. Been driving all day."

She answered with a look. Disbelief. Exhaustion.

The look isn't just killing me, I thought, *it's burying me and planting daisies on top.*

I guess I had noticed increasing evidence of Katrina the farther south I drove, but hadn't realized just how badly the northern towns off the coast had been affected by the storm.

"Mostly locals?" I asked. "Or folks from New Orleans?"

"New Orleans, Waveland, Bay St. Louis, Gulfport. All over."

"I see. Any suggestions on other hotels?" I looked at her shirt for a name tag. There wasn't one.

"Hey, eyes up, *eyes up.*"

"I was looking for your name—forget it."

"It's Chanté. And no, not many rooms this far south. A lot of hotels aren't even reopened yet, so that makes it even harder to handle the load."

"I see."

Women are good at gauging when men feel like idiots. "It's nice of you to travel down to help. We need all we can get."

"Oh, no. I mean, no, I'm not exactly going down to help." I felt so small I could have walked under the stack of newspapers on the counter without having to duck.

"If you'd like, I can ask one of our guests if they wouldn't mind sharing."

"No, no, no, I couldn't do that to someone."

"Sir—"

"It's Luke."

"Luke, most of our guests are sharing already."

"You're kidding?"

"Of course not."

I had no idea what to say. The idea of sharing a room with a complete stranger seemed almost as awkward as assuming there would be a vacancy in the first place.

"Sorry I can't help then. There's water and some donated snacks in the lounge. Help yourself."

I thanked Chanté for her trouble and she looked at me like she thought I was pathetic, or at least that's how I'll remember it. She disappeared into the office behind the counter.

The step-down lounge originally meant to hold breakfasts of free bagels, Danishes, yogurt, and Froot Loops was now filled with sleeping bags, cases of hand sanitizer, and bottled water. Some children played Candy Land at a banquet table. Others huddled on a couch watching *Finding Nemo* on the flat screen that usually ran CNN Headline News.

Six or eight adults had pulled chairs away from other tables and gathered around a youngish-looking couple. The petite woman had cropped black hair and tired eyes. Her husband was a hulk of a man with a buzz cut and scruffy beard. Their somber tones captivated the audience. I wondered if the group had been sharing horror and survival tales all day.

I approached.

"It's completely destroyed," the husband told us. "You haven't seen anything like it, I promise you that. Some of the buildings north of town are just ripped up, maybe fixable, but I doubt it. But everything south of the tracks is gone. Whole neighborhoods. Churches. Stores. All of it's gone. It's like God got mad and looked down at us and just erased us right off His map."

"Now, Sweetheart." His wife wrapped herself around his thick arms. "God didn't do this. He just let it happen. There's always a reason."

Before her husband could answer, another man walked up and joined the conversation. "Where is that? Louisiana? What town?"

"No, right here in Mississippi. Waveland, Mississippi. Buddy, you wouldn't believe what's happened down there. Wouldn't believe it. Surge was over thirty feet."

"Thirty?"

"That's what they're saying. Eye or eyewall or whatever came right over Waveland."

He shook his head and spoke more slowly. "Older folks couldn't get out of the way. A lot of them killed. My guy that runs my auto shop—known him since we played D-line together in high school, my best friend really—he lost his daughter. Drown in her own house. Four years old."

The small crowd quieted even further.

"That just isn't right. That just isn't what's supposed to happen. Drown in her own house?"

He spun a white plastic bottle cap on the tabletop.

"Waveland's the town I grew up in. Met my girl there."

"We've known each other since fourth grade," his wife said, squeezing him again.

"They're saying Waveland lost fifty people. There aren't but ten thousand people down in and 'round town. Tight group, you know?"

The man rubbed his face with both of his giant, callused hands, applying so much anxious energy and pressure I could hear his skin squeak.

"I just wish I could load you all up, take you down there, show you the other stories people aren't talking about. Course I know New Orleans is bad off—*real* bad off—but, people, listen to me, there are tons of towns tore up. Waveland's my home. We've lost it all. Shop's in a pile, house is spread out all over the block, nothing left. Nothing but what we fit in the minivan."

His eyes welled up again. He wiped them with the sleeve of his T-shirt.

A short and sweetly-smiling Hispanic woman stood up and came to give the man a hug. He was almost on his knees when he met her to return the gesture.

"Thank you," he mumbled.

Others came and kindly offered support.

"We're here for you," a woman said.

"He just wiped us off the map," the man repeated.

"It's OK, bud. We're in this together," said another.

"Thanks, guys. Thank you."

I made eye contact with the man. I tried to smile through the pain in my chest and gut.

I returned to the parking lot.

I slept in the car.

♩♩♩

I dreamt of the day Mom first realized she couldn't live without the pills.

Dad sat her down and told her how much he loved her. How much he believed in her. How long he'd stand by her. It amounted to a one-man intervention, and it was even less successful than Dad had hoped.

Mom said no.

Then she ushered him out the door on some needless errand and, after taking another of her naps, called me into the living room.

"Sit down by me, my sweet boy."

"Everything OK, Mom?"

"Yes, yes. All is well. Just sit with me for a minute or two. Your dad's still out and about."

Mom's voice wasn't what it used to be. Once it sparkled and fizzed, like bubbles from my favorite soda. It used to make Dad and me smile just to hear it, even if we were two rooms apart from her. The exact words didn't matter.

Now it sounded like wet bread.

"Luke, I'm not doing well. You know this."

"You need something, Mom? Another blanket?"

"No, dear. I mean . . . I mean I'm not doing well at all. I'm not who I used to be." She stroked my hand. "Am I?"

"I know, Mom. You're sick. You're still grieving about Grandma. I know."

"Is that what your father told you?"

"I guess."

"He's right. I am sad. But I'm also tired and angry."

"At me?"

"Of course not at you, sweetheart."

I wondered how many of her words were being generated by the pills. We sat quietly for a few minutes. I suspected she was editing her thoughts before they became words I wouldn't understand anyway.

"I need you to do me a favor, sweetheart."

"Sure, Mom."

"Live."

"I *am* living."

"Not like this. Live your life, son. Take your dad and be what you two want to be, what you were *meant* to be. Stop sitting around here bringing me blankets and V8s and cards from the school. Go live your life. You're still a child, Luke. *A child.*"

She was right. And this wasn't the first or last time I felt trapped in a conversation ten years too early.

"Your dad is a good man, Luke. But he's stubborn. Talk to him. Go. Be happy. Let me be me. You go be *you*."

I began to cry. "But we love you, Mom. We want you to get better."

"I am getting better, don't you see it?"

No.

"But it's taking time. And I hate seeing you wait around for me, hoping I'll jump up and get back to my life like it used to be before. I don't want you to forget me, Luke. I just want you to get on with your life. Get back to the promise of your future."

I put my head on her chest and she ran her fingers through my hair.

"You're such a talented boy. Such a talented, talented boy."

We sat quietly again for a moment.

"Mom, can I ask you something?"

She was asleep.

Later that night, while I sat in my room strumming my guitar, I heard Mom arguing with Dad in the living room. It ended in a familiar way.

"We're never leaving you," he said.

"Charles—"

"I said we're never leaving you. Never."

CHAPTER
14

My neck was kinked and killing me.

My cell phone was ringing in the passenger's seat and my eyes were adjusting to the light. The screen flashed Jordan's name and cell phone number. I let it go to voice mail.

I opened the door of the rental car, stepped into the Mississippi air, and stretched my arms high above my head. I hadn't slept in my car since a friend talked me into "camping out" early in a parking lot for the privilege of paying a hundred and twenty dollars to walk eighteen ridiculous holes and lose eleven balls on one of the toughest and most prestigious golf courses in the country, Bethpage Black in New York.

I would've given anything to be back at that parking lot instead of at this one in Hattiesburg, Mississippi.

I opened the back door of the car and retrieved my toiletry bag from my duffel. My neck and back argued about which hurt worse.

There were new faces at the registration counter when I walked back into the lobby. The lounge was buzzing with people eating granola bars and drinking fresh juice. In the background, Glenn Beck was on the radio riffing about the recovery and Mayor Nagin. Another movie was playing, one I'd never seen before, and a few of the guests from the night before were gathered again, debating FEMA, Cheney, and whether the levees were blown on purpose.

"You hear about this fella from the Coast Guard?" A man in jam shorts took the floor. "He's in charge now. What's his name?"

"Admiral Allen," someone answered.

"Yeah, that guy is for real, ya'll. Read that thing in the paper over there. This cleanup is back on track, ya'll. The Coast Guard is on the *scene.*"

"Amen, brother!" A woman playfully mocked and raised her hands to the sky. "That's my man right there!"

"That's right, girl. Now let's roll. Kids!" He yelled to two children playing tag in the hallway leading from the lobby. "Load up, we're rolling."

I watched the man say good-bye and thank you to the two employees at the counter. Even from where I stood across the lobby it seemed he had love in his eyes. He gave them each a man-hug—shaking one hand, hugging behind the back with the other.

"Godspeed, friends," he said and walked away. His wife had

already loaded the children in their Trooper. As promised, he gunned it and rolled out in style.

I took a granola bar and a cup of cranberry juice. Only one table had an open seat. A man sat alone nursing a cup of coffee and picking at a dry muffin.

"May I?"

He nodded.

"Busy place, eh?"

"Sure is." He added another cream to his coffee and stirred.

I don't know that I felt like I needed to make small talk, since he clearly wasn't interested, but I did anyway. Maybe it was the two days, a thousand miles alone, and sleeping in the car.

"You coming or going?" I asked him.

"Going home."

"Been here helping out?"

He added yet another cream to his coffee. "Was. Drove down to New Orleans. I'm with FEMA. Though more like a contractor, really." He stirred his coffee. "Now I'm going home."

"What's it like down there?"

"You headed down?"

"I am. Today's day three of my drive from New York."

"Good luck to you."

"That bad?"

"It's everything you've seen on the news, and some of what you've heard."

"I'm Luke, by the way, Luke Millward."

"Bobby." He shook my hand.

"Nice meeting you, Bobby." I unwrapped my granola bar. "So it's bad. Snakes, alligators, all that?"

"Nah, some snakes I imagine, but a lot of that stuff isn't true; it's just rumor. Rumor is the only thing that spreads faster than water or fire. But it's just as dangerous."

Wise man, I thought.

"So what did you see?"

"Ah, now, you don't want to know *half* of what I've seen."

"Actually, I do. I'm a photographer. I'd love to know where to go, where to stay away from."

"What's real and what's not?"

"Bingo." The word seemed out of place as soon as I spoke it.

"It's as bad as it looks on TV. The chaos is dying down because so many people have left the city by now. And because a lot of the holdouts are dying too. It's so hard to get to them in time."

"I can imagine."

Bobby got up and refilled his coffee at the buffet.

"No, Luke. You can't." He picked right up when he returned to his chair.

"Two days ago I was on a boat, clearing out a neighborhood. Marking doors. We came upon a house on the east side, water lapping at the top step. There were six or seven kids on the porch. Cutest little kids. So young. So polite. Sweet kids, every one.

Youngest was just a baby, barely walking; oldest I imagine was probably twelve."

He added a creamer to his fresh coffee.

"There were three of us. We came up alongside the porch and two of us hopped off with life jackets to rescue the kids. Planned to take them in two trips, split up the two oldest kids so they could help. My partner and I got onto the porch and told the kids we were there to help. That everything was all right now."

Another creamer.

"I asked where their parents were. One of the little ones, maybe five years old, said Mom was inside and needed help. Right then the oldest grabbed my arm and led me in the house. The smell . . . man, the smell took me right back to 'Nam. The youngster led me through the family room and around a corner toward a bedroom."

Please be alive, I thought.

"Their mother was on her back in bed. Kid told me she'd been relying on oxygen for a couple years."

Please be alive.

"She was dead." Bobby added a third creamer to his coffee.

I closed my eyes and pictured what it must have been like the night the storm rolled in. Wind threatening to push the house over. Fear in the children's voices as the water rose. Mother reassuring them. "We're going to be fine, children. Everything's gonna be all right. Calm, calm, children, let's pray to God again."

I imagined their thirst as the post-Katrina heat wave baked the roof of the house. I imagined the lies the older siblings had to tell. "Momma will be up soon," they must have said.

"You're a good man," I told Bobby.

"Am I? Because here I am going home. Quitting. I can't see that again. I just can't." His eyes were so distant I wondered if he'd even remember meeting me.

"You came, Bobby. That makes you one of the good ones. One of the *great* ones."

I gave my own story—the reason for the trip, the apprehension, the estrangement from my father, my growing fear that not only was my father dead, but that he'd died in a similarly brutal way.

I stood up, shook Bobby's hand with both of mine, and thanked him for his service in the recovery effort.

"You know what," he said. "Follow me out for a minute."

I trailed him to the parking lot.

Bobby pulled a FEMA construction pass from his dashboard and handed it to me. "Put this on your dash. Trust me," he said, "this'll get you wherever you need to go."

Then he wished me luck recovering my father and resumed his lonely drive home.

♪♪♪

The beginning of the end of the career of noted architect Charles Millward started with an ice sculpture and ended with a shouting match with one of the firm's partners. The firm, the partner said, could only look past so many disappearances, missed deadlines, and embarrassing meetings.

They'd already offered to get him into an exclusive Dallas-area rehab center and foot the bill. His greatest defender in the firm, Kaiser, a recovering alcoholic himself, begged Dad to let him sponsor him in Alcoholics Anonymous.

"I'm fine," Dad said. He repeated that so often I think he actually believed it.

I never did. Not when one drink became two, then three, then four. Not when Dad joked to a room full of colleagues paying a courtesy call after Mom's funeral about taking his own life. And certainly not when we were both left alone in the deadly quiet to cope with the twenty-four-hour loneliness we felt when the house finally cleared of mourners and meatloaf. It's an atmosphere unlike any other, and only those who've lost a loved one from underneath their own roof know it.

My camera never left my side during those early weeks of adjusting to life without my zombie mother constantly readjusting her pillow. I took pictures of the house, Mom's things, bouquets that filled every room, the cemetery.

Dad found his solace and companionship in a bottle.

His guilt and loneliness were things I couldn't understand. Dad told me he loved me and would always be there for me. But according to him, it was time for me to become a man and stop being embarrassed by him. On my eighteenth birthday, he wrote in my card that even though his dreams hadn't all come true, mine still could, and he didn't want to stand in the way.

One night before my final exams, Dad heard me crying in bed and came in smelling like Aquaman and Altoids. I told him it was finally setting in that Mom was going to miss graduation. I told him how much I missed the *old* her, the woman who raised me and loved me no matter the amount of stress I inflicted.

Dad told me in his best impersonation of a functional father, "Mom's legacy to you is early entry into the adult world. Take advantage."

It might have been the best advice he ever gave me.

When Dad arrived drunk for a photo expo in the school library during my senior year, I called a cab, calmly took him outside, and asked him to go home.

"But I want to see your work," Dad stuttered.

"Go. I'll bring the pictures home and show you in the morning."

When Dad stood during graduation and yelled so obnoxiously after my name was called that he drowned out the names of Daniel Moore, Kelly and Jonathan Morrison, and Chucky Muth, I made him apologize to the parents of all three in the parking lot.

Despite the drama, I always told myself the time after Mom's death wasn't entirely wasted. I learned to cook pretty well, sign my father's name, make mortgage payments, deposit his paychecks, do laundry, and apply for scholarships on my own.

I even learned that no amount of pressure would ever make me take a single drink of alcohol. Through all the high school parties, college raves, trips around the world, and high-class banquets, I've never had a taste.

One other good thing came from that year of living alone with Dad. Shortly after he quit his job—or got fired, depending on whose version one cares to believe—I convinced Dad to start playing music again. I told him what I thought the counselors he refused to see would have told him anyway. Music would soothe his soul. Help him cope. Give him purpose. Dad hadn't played the guitar or his sax since Mom started complaining of the noise just before she died. It pained him, but he agreed it was for the best, and buried his instruments in their cases.

I was standing in the doorway of his den when he pulled his prized saxophone out of its case for the first time since Mom passed. His hands shook. The ding caused from the defining moment of my 8th grade year was still visible. Dad had taken it in to be fixed, but the brass never looked quite the same. A thin wrinkle in the bell scowled at me.

Dad cradled the sax in his hands like a newborn and wept.

"It's OK, Dad. Mom would *want* you to play again. It's time."

"I can't." He looked up at me. Unshaven. Disheveled.

"Yes, you can. Play for her. Play for me."

He put his lips to the reed and played a slow blues riff. The sound flooded the room, spilling through the open door to overflow the secret nooks and crannies throughout the house that must have felt like they hadn't been touched by such magic in a lifetime.

When he finished the riff, he looked up at my wet eyes and smiled. He calmly returned the sax to its case. "More tomorrow," he said. "I promise."

Then he drove to the liquor store.

When I was accepted to NYU, Dad flew with me to New York, helped me enroll in school, and stayed sober for a couple of weeks. When I put him on a plane home to Texas, I hugged him and told him how proud I was that he was finally trying to quit drinking, finally ready to get his life back on track.

He soon sold the house, cashed in some investments at great penalty, and sent me money I didn't ask for. Nevertheless I was grateful and told him so. The money was enough to survive quite well as a college student in New York.

Dad moved to Nashville to play music.

It didn't take long for him to find a new liquor store.

CHAPTER
15

They were the longest miles I'd ever driven.

The trip from Hattiesburg to New Orleans was less than two hours, but I felt like I'd never arrive at the city's edge. Downed trees and abandoned cars lined some stretches of the highway, and the temperature seemed to rise a degree with every mile marker I passed.

Someone had spray-painted TURN AROUND in red on a green-and-white mileage sign.

I tuned in to the only AM station I could find and listened as a DJ gave his assessment on the state of the city.

"Oh, yes. Yes, yes, yes, yes, yes. Life is good in the Big Easy, my people. The city is slowly draining back into the rivers and into the blessed lake to our north. Now only sixty percent of our streets are in hiding from the government. That's right, people. Is it possible our great city is in no rush to be saved by *this* government?"

I turned up the radio.

"No, not *this* government, not *this* government that pretended we weren't here just a few weeks ago. Not *this* government, *this* federal government that has no use for a predominantly black city."

I could hear the DJ shuffling papers on his desk.

"No, my people, this city is in no rush to go back to the way it was. Back to being ignored when we're weak and held down when we show strength. No, we will not be ignored again, will we, people? No, we will *not*. This city will dry out. This city will rebuild and recover and restore its spirit in spite of those we elected to lead us. In spite of the agencies that slept through Katrina and only awoke when CNN told them to."

I pulled into a gas station that appeared open, but a cardboard sign on the pumps read: STILL NO FUEL. RIDE A BIKE.

I grinned, took a picture of the sign, and continued listening.

"Now, of course I do read the papers. I see the news. I know that most of our city is gone. Our people scattered about like lost tribes in cities near and far, so far away. But we must gather those tribes, my people. Our mission, the mission for those of us who stayed or who have already returned, is to rebuild a city our brothers and our sisters can return home to. We want our blessed neighbors back, and even our enemies, yes, even that woman who stole your job, or the man who stole your wallet; it doesn't matter. We want them *all* to return. We want to rebuild this city so that it invites them back. New Orleans needs her people back. She needs to heal them . . . Remember this. Without our people, there is no city. Without our city, there is no music. Without music, the world has nothing. Now let's get to work, people. Back after this."

If that man doesn't have a congregation, I thought, *it's a crime.* Then I realized he *did* have a congregation—weekdays from nine to noon. I saved the station on the car's radio presets.

A policeman pulled into the parking lot and walked into the gas station convenience store. I turned off the car and followed him in.

"Officer, can I ask you a question?"

The officer pulled a Red Bull from the drink cooler. "Shoot."

"I'm driving down into the city, trying to get to the French Quarter. What's the best way?"

"What on earth you want to do that for? Hardly nothing open." He turned his back and walked toward a display full of Slim Jims.

"It's for work. Not for fun, obviously."

"What kind of work?"

"I'm a photographer."

He looked me over. "Turn around, kid, there's plenty of ya down there already."

"Actually, I *am* a photographer, but I'm also going to identify my father."

"He died in the storm?"

"Yes, sir."

The officer turned his back again and walked up to the

counter. He pulled a free map from a stand by the register. "Come here."

He opened the map and grabbed a pen tied to a string attached to a donut case. "These roads are still closed." He drew squiggles through a surprising number of lines. "This is the main artery. It's open here and here, closed here. The Quarter is dry, but there's not a real direct route unless you're driving an ambulance or military Hummer. You should be able to get to here." He circled an intersection a few blocks east of the Superdome. "When you get stopped, because you *will* get stopped, tell them you're Coast Guard Auxiliary."

"Thank you. And there's ample parking down there?"

The officer looked at me like I was the biggest idiot he'd ever encountered.

"It'll be tough, young man, but just keep driving around. I think you'll find a spot open up. All those day-tripping, gambling tourists have to go home at some point."

The clerk behind the counter snickered.

"Sorry." The officer looked sincerely embarrassed. "That was wrong." He shook my hand. "Good luck with your father."

"Thanks for the map." I nodded and walked toward the door. But in a simple, insignificant act that made me think of my father, I turned around, took out my wallet, and paid for the officer's Red Bull and Slim Jim.

"God bless you," he said.

Twenty minutes later I found myself navigating side streets and roadblocks. I saw signs and scenes that days earlier had only existed on my television in my comfortable Manhattan studio apartment.

Flooded cars. An abandoned shopping cart filled with personal belongings. Two older men sleeping in the shade under a bridge. At least I assumed they were sleeping. After I took their photos through my open driver's window I realized they could just as easily be dead.

I parked on a residential street that appeared to have the most life. A man and woman dragged a taped-up refrigerator to the street curb. One of their neighbors had already done the same.

I locked my bags in the trunk, put my camera around my neck, stuck my notepad in my back pocket, and double-checked that the photo of Dad was still in my shirt pocket.

Then I set off on foot.

The French Quarter, my father's last employer, *Verses,* Jerome, Dad's fiancée—the existence of whom was a fact I'd forgotten until just then—could wait.

Across the street two women siphoned gas from a powder-blue Grand Prix into a red, five-gallon gas can.

Just a few yards from them crows pecked at what looked like a squirrel. When I passed by, I realized it was a cat with a collar.

Almost every home's windows were boarded up. Some streets had debris pushed to the side, others hadn't been cleared yet.

Helicopters flew overhead almost constantly, a welcome noise in the eerie quiet of the near-deserted city.

I stepped out of the road as two National Guard Hummers chugged by.

Amazingly, sometimes only a block separated the dry streets from the streets under four feet of water.

I walked toward the torn roof of the Superdome. It was as dramatic and as unsettling as it had been on my television set in New York. I recognized the I-10 overpass that had been home to so many live reports, and one of the favorite images for news helicopters to send around the globe. I hadn't expected this double vision: my eyes and mind struggled to process the same scenes and specific geography I'd been seeing on television since the storm.

I took a few pictures of my own.

A blue landscaping tarp that I knew must be shielding an innocent body from the blistering sun.

Children's shoes. A broken megaphone.

I weaved my way to the edge of the French Quarter. Very few of the doors to the clubs and restaurants were open.

Then I heard faint music from the next street up. I picked up my pace and rounded the corner to the right. Three blocks ahead I saw a small group of people moving toward me.

A funeral procession, I thought. *The first since Katrina?*

I noticed immediately that it was not quite the kind of jazz funeral I'd heard or read about. It was a ragtag group, with only a few instruments, no caisson, just a single casket being carried by a couple of men.

I wonder if it's empty.

Along with the casket, there were another half-dozen people moving down the street in their own odd rhythm. I recognized the tune: "Just a Closer Walk with Thee." A few curious National Guardsmen watched from the sidewalk.

I walked halfway down the block, stood in the center of the street, and took some pictures at the highest resolution possible. I couldn't tell exactly how many people there were, or even see their faces very well. Toward the rear of the procession, a woman appeared to be twirling a tattered purple parasol. Even from my distance I could tell they were all dead tired.

I took a few more photos of the surrounding buildings and moved on.

Back on Canal, I marveled at the number of satellite trucks decorated with every network logo on the planet. They hummed with the sound of generators and air conditioners. A reporter prepared for a live shot by scribbling notes on a folded piece of paper, standing on one leg and using his thigh as a desk.

I introduced myself to a man from Pakistan, a resident of St. Bernard's Parish, who'd been selling hats and T-shirts from a table on the street near Harrah's Casino. Now he scavenged for half-empty bottles of water along the curb. He told me the only thing he owned were the shorts on his legs, the sandals on his feet, and a white T-shirt emblazoned with an image of a classic, multicolored Mardi Gras mask. He offered to sell it to me. Instead I took his picture and gave him twenty bucks. His name was Muhammad Saleem.

I walked to the Riverfront Marketplace, a collection of shops at the end of Canal. This was one place where the flooding had been kept in check, but looters gutted many of the stores anyway. Some stole to survive; others stole to stay together. A few stole because they could.

I read the tourist markers along the river. The history of jazz. The food. The swamps. Creoles. The great flood of 1927 and the intentional, controversial explosion of levees that flooded St. Bernard and Plaquemines Parishes but saved the rest of the city.

I wondered how long it would take for there to be a new marker along the boardwalk explaining Katrina.

A white man and woman sat on the steps near the fountain in the Spanish Plaza overlooking the mighty Mississippi. The woman rested her head on the man's lap.

"Hi, folks," I said as I approached.

"Hello." The man's British accent startled me.

"You're from the UK."

"We are." The man made eye contact though his wife's eyes remained closed.

"You're here with a relief organization?"

"No. We're here—we *were* here—on holiday, actually."

"You were here for Katrina then."

He nodded and kissed the top of his wife's head.

The man introduced himself as William Cline and invited me to sit. He told me how he and his wife, Louise, had come to the States for vacation. They visited Las Vegas, planned for three days in New Orleans, and then three more in New York before flying home.

"Then came Katrina," he said. They'd arrived two days before it hit and decided, rather than rush off, they would stay and ride it out. "This is something we'd never see. Why not, we thought. An adventure."

William continued. "We were stopping just up there." He gestured to the Marriott a few blocks up. "We gathered in the lobby the night the storm made landfall." He looked out at the calm Mississippi. "Hard to believe it could be so serene now."

I followed his gaze up and down the river. "I wasn't here. I'm from New York, just down here taking pictures. I arrived an hour or two ago."

The man nodded politely.

"Would you tell me about it?" I asked. "What was it like?"

William tried to describe the hell of Katrina's on-time arrival. There were sounds, he said, that he'd never heard before. Sounds he couldn't give words to. Children clung to their parents in the lobby. Moms and dads tried to lighten the mood by singing or playing games, but the whips and snaps of the windows and doors made it difficult to do anything but pray to God to deliver them. Men used to wearing thousand-dollar suits blended with humble locals. Hotel managers huddled together and pointed at exits and windows, whispering in tones as frightened as the guests'.

"Then we watched the news the next morning and it seemed to us we'd been spared the worst. Sure we walked outside in the bright sunlight and saw damage, but we thought we'd been spared."

"Then you heard about the levees."

"That's correct. The levees went, and we sat in our room watching it all. Almost numbing, you know?"

I know.

"My wife," he finished, "she's having a tough go of it. Been horribly depressed. We've been volunteering at a shelter in an elementary school about ten blocks north. It's hard to see, you know?"

I do.

"We're hoping to catch a flight out tomorrow. Get Lou here to a doctor at home. Get her something to help her sleep. She's not been sleeping a wink, have you, Love?" He stroked her hair with a familiar kind of pure devotion.

"Keep a close eye on her, please," I said. I hoped it didn't sound like I was pleading, but in retrospect it might have.

"Good luck," I added. "My best wishes to you both."

Louise opened her eyes, smiled slightly, and said "Thank you" in the most innocent, kind English accent.

There is no guile in these two, I thought. *No agenda. No selfish, ulterior motives. They breathe charity in its purest form.*

I said good-bye and walked away.

Good luck.

I strolled back up Canal toward Bourbon Street. The city's street vendors wouldn't return for weeks, but a few shop owners gathered to gossip on corners. I listened as I casually walked by. The men made bold predictions about who would reopen and when. One man said he was leaving to meet his family in Houston and would have to be dragged back to New Orleans.

Troops patrolled the streets.

A sign on a souvenir shop said, "Gone fishing in the Ninth."

A white Red Cross tent had been erected in the middle of the street. Empty pallets surrounded the entrance where I imagined thousands of bottles of water must have once been distributed to survivors who hadn't had a drink in days.

I continued down Bourbon to Toulouse and turned right. I tried to picture my father walking up and down these same streets. Had he played on the corners I'd passed, collecting coins and the occasional bill in his velvet-lined saxophone case?

"You." A member of the Coast Guard startled me from my left.

"Yes?"

"You with a group?"

"Group?"

"FEMA, Red Cross, whatever."

"No, I'm a journalist. A photographer."

"Let's see some I.D."

I pulled my license from my wallet and handed it to him.

"Credentials?"

I've got a $3,000 camera hanging around my neck. That good enough?

"Hold on," I said, and dug through my wallet.

"Never mind. Just be careful." The guardsman handed me back my license and moved on.

I walked the final block. My stomach spun when I first saw the darkened neon sign for Verses. I should have expected it, but someone had taped a picture of my father on the door.

He sat with a group of smiling, almost giddy-looking children who were holding instruments of all kinds. Dad held his sax.

In the photo his upper-body was circled in blue felt pen. Above his head were the words: CHARLIE MILLWARD—MISSING.

What hadn't been entirely real before now stared at me in full-color, 8x10, glossy truth.

I opened the door. I heard chatter from upstairs, but the main floor of the club appeared empty. Fifteen tables and scattered chairs crowded the room in the center.

I took a single step inside.

To the right, a thick wooden bar ran from the back of the club almost to the door. Coolers were lined up along half of it. A stack of boxes along one wall read, "Shelled Peanuts." To the left and against the wall sat a platform stage a foot or two off the ground. It held a set of drums and enough chairs for a jazz band.

A woman appeared.

She came from a small room behind the bar. She had light brown skin and her black hair was pulled back in a ponytail. A few strands snuck out on each side and she tucked them behind her ears with her thumb and index finger. Her dark eyes spoke of both fatigue *and* resilience. Her mouth was the most rare kind, the one that could say, "I'm happy," even if she wasn't talking or even smiling. She wore khaki cotton shorts that almost hit her knees and a T-shirt that said

VISIT VERSES

FRENCH QUARTER, NEW ORLEANS

CENTER OF THE UNIVERSE

She wore heavy-looking hiking boots and midankle socks with a Nike Swoosh on the cuff.

Her earrings were small gold hoops that looked like they had been made specifically for her skin color.

Her name was Bela.

PART 2

CHAPTER
16

Her voice was as beautiful as her name.

My palms were actually a little sweaty.

"Can I help you?" she asked.

If Jessica Alba had a better-looking sister, it could be Bela. As I appreciated her striking good looks, I predicted one of her parents was Latino and the other Caucasian.

"Luke Millward." I finally extended my hand.

She took it reluctantly but gave a firm shake.

"Bela Cruz."

"I'm looking for Jerome," I said. I noticed a delicate gold chain dangling a cross against her neck.

"Not here. Came back with us a little while ago then disappeared again."

"Any idea how long until he'll be back?"

"None."

"Can I wait here?"

She stepped aside and gestured into the club.

"Nice place," I said, and if there had been a beer bottle within reach I would have broken it over my head as soon as the words left my mouth.

"Thanks, I guess."

"I just meant, nice job keeping things running, being open for people."

"We're not *open,* not for actual business anyway. We're just offering support to some people in the Quarter."

"The *French* Quarter."

"Mm-hmm," she answered.

I'd never heard "mm-hmm" done with such sarcasm.

"We're a staging area of sorts. Club's owner has opened up to others in the Quarter." She curled her lips just enough to qualify as a smile. "The *French* Quarter. We've got water, some food still in the back we can cook up, packaged snacks, sanitizing wipes, a generator, and some alcohol. But not much else."

"And an open door, most importantly."

"True," she said and began slicing open cardboard boxes with a box cutter.

I zigzagged around supplies, small round tables, and scattered bentwood chairs to a wall filled with photos of famous patrons enjoying themselves at Verses: Nicolas Cage, Adam Sandler, John Goodman, Spike Lee, Wynton Marsalis, Ray Nagin, and New

York City's very own Naked Cowboy in his bright-white jockeys and waxed chest.

"Naked Cowboy, huh? Didn't know he traveled outside of New York. I see him in Times Square pretty much year-round."

Bela stood abruptly and seemed to finally notice my camera. "You're from New York?"

"Yes, I am, in fact." I was both impressed *and* curious.

"Wait here." Bela climbed a spiral staircase to the second floor and the noise from the crowd upstairs quieted to something only slightly louder than sign language.

Uh-oh. I'd either walked into a reality show or Bela had news about my father. Or both. I picked a barstool and sat.

Moments later a tall, lean African-American woman followed Bela back down the stairs. The woman approached me, but Bela walked straight out the door.

The woman wore no makeup and had a thin scar on her left cheek that ran almost from the bottom of her nose to her temple. Even still, she had the look of a woman who didn't need makeup to attract attention. "Are you Luke?"

"Yes, ma'am." I stood and reached out my hand, but she pulled me into a hug. After a long, uncomfortable embrace, at least for one of us, she kissed my left cheek and let me go.

"I'm your father's fiancée."

"Jez."

"That's right. Short for Jezebel. My brother tell you?"

135

Who else? "That's right," I said politely.

"Bela's gone to find him."

I asked the most obvious question next. The one I should have asked Jessica Alba as soon as I walked in the door instead of admiring her legs. "Have you seen or found my father?"

"Let's wait for Jerome. He's just around the corner."

Dad's dead, I thought. I wondered if my mother was waiting for Dad the way he'd dreamed.

I breathed deeply and looked at the woman who would have been his second wife. She wore faded blue jeans, scuffed tennis shoes, and a green tank top. She was confident. Attractive and fit. Stylish. Everything Dad hadn't been since the year Mom passed away.

"How did you and my father meet?"

Before answering, she took a seat next to me at the bar. "We met here. I do the bookkeeping for the club and your dad walked in seven months ago—almost eight—looking for gigs. Let's just say we didn't have any spots immediately, but I was motivated to keep him here."

Only then did I notice just how tired and red her eyes looked.

"You're a bookkeeper?"

"Accountant, to be precise. . . . You look incredulous."

"No, no, not at all."

"It's OK. Let me guess. You talked to my brother on the phone and could barely understand him." She cocked her head to get a better view at the dumb look on my face. "Then you arrive here and find his educated, well-spoken sister. You're not the first to wonder if one of us is adopted."

"I really didn't mean—"

"Hush. Quit all that white-boy worrying over there."

I laughed.

She did too. "We're from New Awlins. Born and bred. I went to LSU and earned a masters of accounting. Math was my thing growing up. I don't know what sparked it but I always loved numbers. And Jerome's thing, his passion, was always music. *Is* music."

"A nice partnership then."

"Uh-huh. We don't own the club, but we might as well. Jerome handles all the music and lives upstairs in an apartment on the back side of the building. I do the books, Bela helps run the bar when she can. And we have the requisite barkeeps, bouncers, a couple cooks . . ."

I must have drifted off because the next thing I heard was, "You OK?"

"I'm sorry, yes. Forgive me, it's just . . . so *odd* to think of you and my father. A couple. Getting married."

"Because I'm black?"

"No, because Dad was a drunk."

She laughed even harder this time and playfully wagged her long finger at me. She had a bright, wide smile. As her pleasant laugh ebbed, Jerome appeared at the front door.

Bela followed him in.

"Jerome, this is Luke," Jez said. "Charlie's boy."

"Charlie?" I said, shaking Jerome's hand.

"We started callin' 'im that after he got a spot in the band. He took to it."

"What can you tell me? Has he been recovered or identified?" I hadn't practiced that line, but now I wished I had.

"Sit down, son." Jerome led me back to my barstool and, with a subtle nod, sent his sister and Bela upstairs.

I noticed that Bela watched me closely until she cleared the top of the stairs.

"He's gone, isn't he?"

Jerome reached over the bar and pulled two warm beers off a hidden shelf. He put one in front of me.

"No thanks," I said.

"That's right, I remember. You don't drink a lick."

"Dad told you."

"Yes, sir, he did. Good for you." He opened his beer and took a long drink. "He was proud of you for that. That you decided to be a, what do they call that?"

"Teetotaler. But it's not a big deal; I just don't drink."

"Teetotaler. That's right. Dumb word—teetotaler." He said the word with disdain. "Makes me think of tea. Why ain't it *beer*-totaler?"

I grinned broadly, despite, or maybe *because* of the nerves.

Jerome took another swig of his warm beer. "Son, we don't know 'bout your father yet."

I exhaled. *Is this relief?*

"No word. We got people all over the city lookin', checkin' shelters, askin' 'round."

"I'm relieved," I mustered.

"Yeah?"

"Of course. I drove down here, didn't I?"

Jerome's face shone wisdom. "That's right, you did." He finished his beer. "You didn't exactly rush though, did you, son?"

"I really couldn't." It was the best I could come up with.

He stared right through me. "You take the long way?"

"Pardon me?"

"Nothin'. You're here. We're happy for you. Happy for your dad, too."

"You think he's alive?"

"For now I'm talkin' like he is. Cause we're goin' to find 'im, son, one way or another. And you're goin' to help us."

"All right."

"Good."

"Is there a hotel open yet? I've got nowhere to stay."

"Nothin' in the city. You can go north across the lake and find somethin', maybe, but rooms are tight right now. But we got you all set. Got a sofa bed upstairs."

"Here?"

"That's right. Cause I didn't say upstairs someplace else, did I?"

"No, sir, I couldn't put someone out, but I'm really grateful, truly—"

"You sound like Charlie." He stood up and stomped on his beer can, crushing it flat, and then flung it like a Frisbee toward a tall black trash can in the corner. The can bounced off the wall and fell in. "We have the will and the room, Charlie Millward's boy. You'll stay here. Go back to your car, get your belongin's or bags or whatever you brought, and come back before dark. Curfew's in effect but ignore anythin' you hear overnight. Some of the reporters hangin' around have been comin' by late for a drink."

"Really?"

"That's need-to-know. Got it?"

I nodded.

"Good on you. Tomorrow we'll get to work."

I had no desire to trudge back to my car.

As if rehearsed, Bela and Jez made their way down the stairs and into the conversation. Jez looked like she'd been crying again.

"Jez, Luke's goin' to be our guest upstairs. Would you mind settin' up the gray couch for 'im?"

"Happy to," Jez answered.

"Bela. Would you mind walkin' with Luke back down to his car so he can get his things?"

"Sure, Jerome."

"Great," I said eagerly. "Let's go."

CHAPTER
17

Bela's bronze legs moved faster than mine did.

"Wait up, you're killing me."

"Sorry, Luke," she said as we turned onto Canal. "Used to walking fast, I guess."

I picked up the pace and walked at her side.

"Tell me again where you're parked?"

I was beginning to lose my breath; I calculated in my head the last time I'd been to the gym. "A mile from the Superdome. Garden District, I think."

"You didn't write it down? Or take a picture?"

That would have been an excellent idea, I thought. "No, no, I'll remember it."

"Uh-huh."

Is she walking even faster?

We walked, mostly in silence, until we neared the area where I remembered parking the car. In the gray light of the September evening, I saw the two men still sleeping under a bridge and accepted that their sleep was eternal. I hoped they weren't too far from the main streets to be noticed and recovered by the Red Cross, FEMA, or anyone else with body bags. I also wondered if they had worried children somewhere.

A moment later we reached my car. I removed my duffel and laptop bags from the trunk. I slung my camera bag over my shoulder.

"Is that everything?" Bela asked.

"Think so."

"I don't want to stress you out, Luke, but there aren't many dry cars down here. So make sure there's nothing valuable here, because it's a pretty attractive target."

"For looters? Really? A cheap rental car?"

"It's survival. That backseat would be a welcome place for someone to sleep."

"True enough."

"You got the rental insurance, right?"

Whoops. "Of course."

Bela's eyebrows drew together and she reached out for a hand-written note that had been slipped under one of the wiper blades. She read it out loud in the fading light.

"Whoever you are, you're brave (or stupid) to leave a FEMA car unattended because you aren't the most popular four-letters in town right now. We wanted to leave you a not-so-friendly spray-painted

message telling you where to go but then we noticed the pass is for FEMA Construction—the good guys. So . . . thanks for coming. Thanks for staying. Thank you for helping us recover."

She gently folded the note and handed it to me. Then she tapped the window above the FEMA Construction pass. "Looks like this is better than rental insurance."

I swallowed past a sudden lump in my throat and carefully slipped the note into my wallet, grateful that small miracles were still happening in the Big Easy.

Bela reached over and took the laptop bag from me. "Here, I got that."

We began to follow our route back to Verses, each block bringing darker shades of gray and a faster pace.

"So it's really unsafe down here after dark?"

"Not exactly *unsafe,* not like the wrong-side-of-town unsafe. There's just a lot of desperation down here, everywhere really. Not many people left in the city, but the ones who stayed are trying to survive."

"What about the evacuation? Why aren't they forcing you out?"

"We've held out pretty well because they have more important things to do right now than chase out locals."

"Especially locals trying to assist."

"Correct. And they know they can't legally force us off our property anyway. It's mostly rhetoric. Jerome's had that argument a few times already."

"So why did you stay? And Jerome and Jez and the others?"

"I guess because we knew if we got on a bus we might never come back. And we had too many friends not accounted for yet. Neighbors. A few employees."

We crossed Canal Street and heard a howling wail from down an alley. In the fading light it appeared a man was beating a dog with something.

"Hey! Hey!" I yelled. "Stop!"

"Don't, Luke." Bela grabbed my forearm.

"That guy down there—he's killing that dog!"

"I see him. The animal is probably sick. Let's go."

"You're not—"

"Let's go, Luke. He's doing the dog a favor. Trust me. I watched a guy kill a rabid dog with a clock radio a few days ago."

A clock radio? I thought. In any other setting I might have called her a liar. But in that place, on that street, I had no doubt she had seen just such a thing.

As we walked away, the dog's wails turned to whimpers. Then silence. I looked over my shoulder as the man exited the alley and sat on the curb. It was too dark to be certain, but I was sure he was crying.

I'd never felt so out of place and disoriented.

I walked faster.

Just a few blocks later we walked back through the front door of Verses. The lights were on.

"Power's on," I said.

"Won't last. It's been on and off since the storm." Bela picked up two flashlights off the bar. "Just in case." She handed me one as we climbed the staircase. She flipped a light switch at the top of the stairs.

"You'll leave that flashlight with me?"

"Scared of the dark?" she teased.

"No, just can't see a thing. If the lights go out, I'll kill myself falling down the stairs."

She didn't laugh. "Of course I'll leave it." She pointed with her flashlight at a couch pushed up against the wall between the top of the stairs and the head of a hallway. There was a pillow at one end of the sofa and a blanket folded at the other. "This is you. No door, I'm afraid, but roomy."

"How about the rest of you?"

"There are a couple other rooms down there." She nodded toward the hallway. "A pretty big one that way—a few are staying in there on the floor." She pointed her flashlight the other direction.

"I don't need the couch, Bela. I'm grateful but the floor would be fine, really."

"Relax. Jerome said the gray couch was yours." She set my laptop bag by my feet.

"Thank you."

"You're welcome."

I sat on one end of the couch and let myself settle into the soft, worn cushions. Whatever energy I'd had left fled into the unknown around me. "Who else stays here, if I can ask?"

"May I?" she asked as she sat.

On the opposite end of the couch Bela also melted into the comfortable cushions. She rested her head on the back of the couch, sighed, and stretched her legs out into the room. "Hard to say right now, people are coming and going. Jerome has his place, an apartment you can get to from outside. There's an office up here, too."

"And Jerome said my dad lived in the Lower Ninth?"

"That's right. Jez lived down there, too."

"With him?"

"Oh, no. Your dad wouldn't let her move in until they got married."

"Hmm. Interesting. Is his place still standing?"

"I hear it is. I haven't seen for myself. But if it is, it's still flooded. Too bad, it was a pretty nice place, actually."

"I didn't realize there were nice places in the Ninth Ward. The news made it sound like mostly projects."

"The Ninth Ward is actually broken into the Upper and Lower, everything above or west of the canal is the Upper. And there are no housing projects in the Lower, if you can believe that. One of the few areas in the city without them."

"Interesting."

"There's plenty of poor folks over there, that's true. But they're still home owners, a lot of them anyway. I haven't seen the news much lately, but I bet they make it sound like a ghetto."

I nodded, but she was looking the other direction. "I guess they do," I said. "Some of them anyway."

"It's not the Garden District," Bela offered. "But a lot of good people live there. Some well-known people in the city, musicians, business owners, artists, good families. Some whites, blacks, in-betweens like me, some foreigners. Mostly black, obviously, like most of the city, but more a melting pot than you'd believe."

"How about you? Where do you live?"

"I live a few blocks away in a cozy apartment. No lights or water right now. But it's dry. Thank the Lord."

"Cozy?"

"Small." She smiled at me, but before I could fully appreciate it, the lights went out. "And there they go. Probably won't see power again through the night."

We sat in the darkness. I wondered if she was still smiling. "And you work here full-time?" I asked.

"Hours vary, but usually I'll pull forty-plus-hour weeks. I'm a student at Tulane, so my schedule is all over the place." Her voice began to soften and her cadence slow. It reminded me of how tired I was, too.

"You're a student?"

"Yeah, I know, I'm old. It's taken me a while."

"I wasn't—"

"Relax," she interrupted. "It's OK. I'm a grad student. I've been working on a masters in social work."

"Good for you."

"Thanks. It will be worth it one day. That's what they tell me anyway."

"You do your undergrad there, too?"

"Sure did. Bounced around from job to job, depending on where I was living. Finally found a great—that means *cheap,* by the way—place down here in the Quarter. Then your dad and Jez got me this job."

"Really?"

"Sure did. I won't bore you with the details, embarrassing details if we're being honest, but the two of them were on a date down by the river at a place were I was waiting tables. Not very well, apparently, because I got fired."

"And they were there?"

"Sure were. They were at the next table over the very night I got canned."

"You got fired while you were on a shift?" I asked.

"Didn't I say no embarrassing details?"

"Apologies."

She took a moment before continuing. "I made a mistake. The customer got really upset. I lost my cool. Then I made a bigger mistake. The guy got even more upset. The manager came out and he lost *his* cool. He fired me."

"And people saw."

"Lots of people saw. Including Charlie and Jez. They came running after me, each put an arm around me, and offered me a job here. I have no idea what they saw in me, but I'm grateful they saw something. The next day I showed up downstairs and they put me to work. First time I've ever really cared about the people I worked with."

"Interesting."

"Sure is," she said.

"But you're not from New Orleans?"

"You need to start saying it right. Everyone down here says, 'New Awlins.'"

"Won't I look stupid trying to talk like the natives?"

"Probably."

"Gee, thanks."

"So you're not from New *Awlins?*"

She smiled. "Nope—Mesa, Arizona. It's in the Phoenix area. My dad was born in Mexico and my mom's from LA. They're sort of an odd couple who fell in love."

Bingo, I thought. "Do you know Jessica Alba?"

A door opened downstairs.

"Who's here?" It didn't matter that I'd only met him late that afternoon, Jerome's booming voice was impossible to mistake for anyone else's.

"Up here," Bela called.

"He up there?"

"Yes, sir. He's settling in."

"You all need anythin'?"

"We're all right, Jerome. I'm headed home soon."

"OK then. Be careful; have the kid walk you."

"I'll be OK, Jerome."

"He'll walk you," Jerome said firmly.

"All right."

"Jez is waitin' on me at the hostel 'round the corner. Tryin' to fix a generator." He paused. "He know anythin' 'bout generators?"

She whisper-giggled. "You know he's still awake, right, Jerome?"

Awkward silence.

"You know anything 'bout 'em?"

"No, sir. If it's not a digital camera or a laptop I'm afraid I'm not much help."

"Thanks anyway."

The door shut and I was sure I heard Jerome say that a no would have sufficed. Bela and I sat quietly for a few moments.

"He's harmless," she finally said.

"Seems like a good man."

"The best."

"Jerome says he knew my father well. Did you?"

"Not as well as Jez, of course, but I think I got to know him pretty well pretty fast."

"Because he got you your job?"

"You ask a lot of questions." From the sound of her voice I could tell she was looking in my direction.

"I apologize."

"Don't worry about it. Your dad had my back, and I appreciated that more than he knew. He was honest, sincere, someone you could talk to. Not just me though, he was good to everyone here at Verses."

"Understood."

Two figures climbed the stairs and passed by the couch. "Heya Bela," one of them greeted her without stopping.

"Hi, Tater. Hi there, Hamp. Hanging in?"

"Mm-hmm."

The two walked down the hallway to the larger bedroom. They breezed a trail of stench that lasted long after the door shut.

"Friends of Jerome's?"

"Friends of the club. . . . They've been searching attics."

"Oh." I felt guilty for even noticing the smell.

"Luke, you haven't talked to your dad lately, have you?"

"Not since he moved to New Orleans, no."

"I thought so."

"Why?"

She didn't answer.

"Our relationship was complicated," I said. "Dad would call, ask for something, then go into witness protection for months at a time. It seemed that way anyway. Then I'd get a call out of the blue, often from somewhere new. He'd followed some band, a card game, whatever."

"I see," Bela offered.

"Let me guess. I can only imagine he was trying to get sober again, right?"

"You know what, it's late." Her voice moved away from me again. "I better get out of here."

She stood.

I followed.

She led me down the stairs and out of the club. We walked briskly through the near-dark toward her place. Only about half the streetlights appeared to be working. Along the way, Bela pointed out places she'd eaten and places Dad had played.

We got stopped by police, twice, the second time just in front of her apartment building. I wished the walk had been just a few blocks farther.

"You OK then?" I asked Bela after the police officer left us and rounded the corner.

"Sure am. Can you get back?"

"I think so."

She reminded me of the route back anyway.

"Thank you for everything," I said, sticking out my hand.

She shook it firmly. Even bathed in the yellowish glow from

the streetlight she had a beautiful presence I could hardly look away from.

"I'll see you tomorrow? Or do you have school?" I asked.

"There is no school right now, Luke. Tulane's closed. Everything's closed."

"I'm such an idiot. I apologize."

"Don't. We're all out of our element right now. Get some rest. There's a bathroom at the end of the hall at the club. No shower, but a sink and a toilet. And don't drink the water. There's plenty of bottled water downstairs. Help yourself."

"Thanks."

The woman I'd met only a few hours ago smiled and entered her building.

The streetlight above me went dark.

I didn't so much walk back as I jogged. Fast.

The bottles of water were easy to find, and I also helped myself to a package of beef jerky and some saltines. I used the restroom, kicked off my shoes, pulled my hand sanitizer from my bag, and stretched out on the couch in my clothes. I wondered when I'd shower again, when I'd eat a full meal, how long it would take to find my father, and how I'd feel if and when I stood over his body and said, "That's him."

Then I realized I'd forgotten to call Jordan since the McDonald's in Knoxville.

CHAPTER
18

Jezebel was cursing like a sailor.

"Get out! We're not interested. *We—are—not—interested.*"

I sat up on the couch and checked my watch: 9:18. I couldn't believe I'd slept so late. I rubbed my eyes, remembered the time- zone difference, and moved my watch back an hour.

"Listen, boys," Jez continued loudly from downstairs. "You've got about ten seconds before I stand on the street and scream for my life. Dare me?"

I hopped off the sofa and walked down the stairs. A camera crew of three stood just inside the door. They mumbled something to one another in French, swore at Jez using two words that translated perfectly, and walked out.

"What's wrong?"

"Hey, Luke." Jez shut the door behind the Frenchmen. "Some clowns wanted to shoot footage inside the club, interview me, whatever. We're not interested."

I stretched my arms high above my head and yawned.

"You sleep all right?"

"Sure, considering. I'm actually surprised I slept so late."

"Remember, the city is a dead zone, especially with no electricity all night." She walked back behind the bar. "It's back on now. You hungry?"

"I'm OK."

"Quit that fibbing, you must be starving. I've got Pop-Tarts, MREs, toast, Spam."

"Door number one sounds delicious."

Jez reached under the bar and retrieved a package of S'more's-flavored Pop-Tarts. "Enjoy." She slid them to me. "Follow me." She led me to one of the tables in a back room. We sat across from one another.

"People were eating dinner here not ten days ago." She didn't seem to be talking to me.

"They'll come back, right?"

"Maybe." She twisted her diamond engagement ring.

I opened my Pop-Tarts and broke one in half. "S'more?"

Jez smiled. "No, thanks, I ate a bagel already. Got a stash hidden."

I put the bite in my mouth. *Surprisingly delicious,* I thought. While I was savoring my second bite, Jez stood and brought me back a bottle of water. "Thanks," I said sincerely, though I'd had enough water the last twenty-four hours to fill a small pond. I was instantly grateful I'd kept that to myself.

"So tell me, Jezebel. What's the next step?"

"It's Jez," she said. "Always Jez."

"Understood."

"Tater and Hamp are back with the Auxiliaries going house to house."

"Coast Guard Auxiliaries?"

"That's them. About the best thing going down here."

"Are they still finding people?"

"Alive or dead?" Jez asked.

"Both, I guess."

"Lots of dead. Not many alive anymore, though another team did find a man and his wife up in an attic. He was alive; she wasn't."

"What must it be like to watch your wife die?" I mused quietly.

She looked at me and continued. "Jerome and the cousins are feeding some pets."

"Pets?"

"That's right. Pets. Most people had to leave their dogs, cats, whatever, behind. Wouldn't let them on the buses. Some of the guys have been risking a lot to get back in the neighborhoods to get the critters food."

"All for nothing?"

"Not exactly. They do it in exchange for batteries, cigarettes, whatever food isn't spoiled, you know."

"Fascinating."

"You could call it that. But I can tell you firsthand that Jerome would be out there helping these people with their animals whether he got something for it or not. That's Jerome. He loves helping—whatever, whoever, two legs, four paws, it doesn't matter."

"Is that how he met my father?"

She reached over and broke off a corner of my second Pop-Tart. "Now that, Luke Millward, is a segue." She popped the piece in her mouth. "That's one way to think of it, but your dad wasn't a charity case, Luke."

"No?"

"No. He came here looking for work, but he could play. Played piano, sax, guitar, some trumpet. He could *play*." Unlike the day before, this time I saw the tears for myself.

"You loved him."

"I sure did. I sure did." She pulled a balled-up napkin from her pocket and wiped her eyes. "Your dad was a good soul. And, oh, *oh,* when he played . . . I never heard music like that before."

I broke the rest of my second Pop-Tart in half and handed it to her. This time she accepted.

"Your dad showed up here one night at closing time. I was running around trying to account for some missing cash. But I remember your Charlie was carrying his sax case—I'll never forget that. So he asks to see the owner or manager. It was really quiet in here for some reason that night. Maybe there was a football game going on—I don't recall. But it was slow. Someone got Jerome from the back and he told your dad the owner was out of town. Truth is, Mr. Hunt is always out of town. Has a place up north on the other side of the lake—probably dry as the desert right now—but he's hardly in it. Travels all over. Says he likes to see things. I think he's just bored. Lonely."

I twisted the cap off my water and washed down my breakfast.

"Jerome says he's the closest thing to a manager working and asks Charlie what he needs. Your dad shakes his hand, tells him he had a premonition—"

"A dream."

"No, he said *premonition.* He'd had a premonition that he was supposed to come here looking for work. Wanted to play with the boys, but offered to work in the kitchen, sweep floors, whatever. My brother told him they didn't have much to offer, but he'd let him work that night cleaning up the place in exchange for a meal and a drink. . . . Oh, Luke, your dad looked hurt. Looked like he'd been punched in the stomach. He said no thanks to the meal and the drink and started to leave. But when Jerome turned around, walking back behind the bar, your dad stopped and pulled that sax out. He played music, Luke, such music. Music like I've always imagined the Lord listens to on Friday nights when He gathers His children who have already returned home." Jez wiped her nose again. "I don't know why I'm surprised to be crying now; I cried that night too. I'm telling you, your dad bled his heart through that saxophone."

I knew exactly what she meant. I'd heard Dad play like that before, get into his rhythm and play so effortlessly you wondered where the music was really coming from.

"Jerome and the others came out. Michael, Schubert, Heath, even my niece Angela who was working that night, too. They all came out with their jaws hanging open. Now remember, Luke, these people live in Louisiana. They know good music like no one you've ever met. Then Jerome started asking questions. How long had he been playing? Did he write? Where was he from? Your dad told him everything."

"Everything?"

"If by 'everything' you're meaning everything about you, your mother, his problems, then yes. Everything."

"Sounds like Dad, leaving nothing to the imagination. That's his typical first impression."

"I fell for your dad that night. Crazy, I know. White guy walks in, probably two inches shorter than me, hasn't shaved for a couple weeks. Everything about him said, 'Run, Jez! Get on your Jackie Joyners and run from this man!'"

I couldn't help but laugh.

"I was spinning my wheels before your dad walked through

that door. I'd been praying for traction, for change. Your dad was it. He was my pivot point."

That sounded like something Larry Gorton would say.

"I'm telling you, the first time our eyes met, I knew he had a heart of gold." She looked at me. "You knew that, too, didn't you?"

Undeniable, I thought. "I guess he did. He was always good to me growing up. But he was never the same after my mother died."

"That was difficult on him."

"And me."

Jez looked up and said hello to two men who came in and walked behind the bar. They poured themselves whiskeys. "Regulars," Jez said to me. "Holdouts like us. They're not leaving unless they're tied up and dragged out of town."

I was still thinking about my mother.

"Sugar, I know. Hard to be a kid and see your mother give up like that. How many times had you heard her say, 'Don't give up, son, don't give up.'"

A million.

"Plenty I bet. That's what mothers do. Dads, too, if they're around. Then sometimes—and it's tragic for everyone—sometimes they can't follow their own advice."

I took another drink of water. "Did you know I played tennis my freshman year of high school?"

Jez looked as surprised at hearing me say it as I was for actually saying it. "No," she said simply.

"I wasn't officially on the team, but we'd play after school and I was always looking for a match. My best friend back then was Jon, and he and I played doubles. He was better than I was, but we played together anyway. I don't know why, but I let him talk me into signing up for a city-wide tournament."

Jezebel listened to me like this was the most important story she'd ever heard.

"I remember when the bracket was posted on the community bulletin board outside the courts. We practically jumped up and down at our first-round matchup: Millward and Swinson versus Hyatt and Dysart. Really? Hyatt and Dysart? We knew those guys. We knew we could take them. In fact I recall thinking, 'At least we'll get out of the first round. We won't be embarrassed. And I won't let my partner down.'"

I saw Jez grab the napkin again and wipe her eyes.

"Match day came. We won the first set, lost the second, went to a third-set tiebreaker. I was playing net during the first game of that final set. Dysart ripped a forehand to my right, and I reached out to stab at it and biffed it on the court."

Jez put her hand to her mouth.

"I laid there on the court. I could feel my right knee bleeding. I was so embarrassed. I could tell my partner had somehow reached the ball behind me and hit it back over the net. Then I heard my dad yell, 'Get up!' So I did. . . . The ball came back to me a couple shots later and I hit a nifty drop shot. We won the point."

"Ha! Wonderful! And then you won the match."

"No. We got beat."

She giggled. "I'm so sorry. I'm so sorry those two boys beat you after all that inspiration."

"They weren't boys."

"Men?"

"Girls."

She wasn't giggling anymore. She was laughing so hard I thought she'd need an oxygen tank.

"Great story, Luke. You tell them like your dad."

With that the door opened again.

Bela.

"Hi, sweetheart," Jez said.

"Morning. Hi, Luke."

"Hey," I said, and remembered with a pang that I still needed to call Jordan.

"What's up this morning?" Bela asked. "Any news?"

"Jerome's out on pet duty. I expect him back soon. Jason and Chad are out looking for more MREs." Jez turned to me as if knowing I was curious. "Those MREs are being left around. The guys have been collecting the ones that obviously don't belong to anyone and bringing them back here. We've sort of become a general store. All barter."

She looked back at Bela. "How about you?"

"I'm here for whatever you need. Actually, could I talk to you for a minute?"

Jez stood and followed Bela out onto the street. I was curious, but saw the opportunity to head upstairs and get ready for the day. I changed my clothes, watered down my hair and brushed my teeth with leftover bottled water. My cell phone was where I'd left it last night and I stuck it in my front pocket, silently pledging to call Jordan when I knew where my day would take me.

I grabbed my camera bag and returned downstairs. Bela and Jez were back inside. Bela was holding three packs of cigarettes.

"Luke, Bela met a police officer from Tennessee who said he'd help drive you around this morning in exchange for cigarettes."

"Really?" I asked.

"General store," she replied with a smile. "Sound good?"

"Excellent. I'm looking forward to finding some answers."

Jez looked at Bela. "We know. We all are. Be safe, you two."

Safety never seemed so relative.

CHAPTER
19

The light outside was blinding. The heat was worse.

After the darkness of Verses, it felt like we'd stepped onto the surface of the sun. It had to have been ninety degrees already.

"It's been like this since the storm cleared," Bela said as we walked down the sidewalk toward Canal.

"I thought it was *always* this hot down here. Sure was growing up in Dallas."

"It's hot, yes, but not like this. This has been brutal on us. I bet the city lost more people from the heat than the water." She hesitated. "Who knows. I have no idea if that's true. I hate to speculate."

I pictured the two dead men under the bridge.

The image was forced from my mind by the vibrating cell phone in my pocket. I removed it and checked the caller ID: JORDAN CELL.

"You're lucky that rang," Bela said. "Calls are sparse coming in, almost none are getting out anymore." She looked at my face. "We can stop so you can answer it. I'd hate to have the signal fade."

"Thanks." I flipped the phone open. "Hi, this is Luke."

"Luke. You OK? You make it?"

"Yes, I'm fine. Made it yesterday late."

Bela took a few steps away to read a menu posted in a glass case for a restaurant that wasn't open.

"You didn't call. I started to worry." Jordan took a deep breath. "Bad time?"

"Not at all. What's new up there?"

"One closing fell through. The wife wasn't a citizen and their bank dumped the loan. Back to square one."

"That's lousy."

"Yeah, but I got another listing, place over on Bleaker. What goes around—"

"Comes around," I finished.

"Karma."

A man approached Bela on the sidewalk.

"How about your dad? I didn't really call to talk real estate."

"No news. We're going out right now to see what we can find."

A beat passed.

"What's it like?"

"The city?"

"Yeah."

"A war zone."

"That's definitely what it looks like on TV."

"It's even worse on the ground," I said and noticed the man Bela had been talking to walking away.

"You met the guy who called?"

"Jerome." Bela looked my way at the mention of his name.

"Good guy?"

"The best."

"Oh, good. . . . So how long do you think it will be before you know something?"

"I wish I knew. Communication is horrible. I'm told cell phones aren't reliable at all and calls out are impossible. Incoming are hit-and-miss."

"I know." She sighed. "I've been trying all morning."

"I'm sorry. Keep trying when you need to reach me. Don't give up."

"I won't."

"I better get going. My guide is standing here waiting for me."

"They got you a guide?"

"Sort of. Someone I met at the club."

"Please be safe."

"We will."

"Try to call?"

"I will, but if you don't hear from me, try my cell anytime. Hopefully you'll get through."

"All right then. I miss you, Luke."

"You too." I did.

"Be safe."

"Thanks, we'll talk soon."

I hung up and tucked the phone back in my pocket.

"Girlfriend?" Bela asked as we began walking again.

"How did you know it wasn't my wife?"

"Your dad said you never married."

"I see. What else did he tell you?" It sounded much more playful than I meant it to. I was genuinely curious.

Bela shrugged. "Your dad liked to talk."

"Really?"

"Sure he did. You just had to listen."

Ouch. I wondered if he'd told her about his last call from Austin.

We walked quietly until we reached Canal Street. She looked left then right. According to Bela, Canal was the widest roadway in America that was called a street and not a highway, boulevard, or avenue. That day it could accurately be called a sea of news trucks, military vehicles, and trash. A police officer to our right waved and caught Bela's attention.

"Here we go," she said. We jogged across the street and Bela introduced me to Officer Rostron of Memphis, Tennessee. He was also, apparently, a bodybuilder. His arms were bigger than the telephone pole he leaned against.

"Pleasure," he said, shaking my hand firmly. Very firmly.

Bela handed him the cigarettes. He slid one pack into his shirt pocket and the others into the left and right pockets of his pants. "The funny thing? I don't even smoke"—he smiled—"but these will get me something good. Maybe even a night off to catch some sleep. I'm doggin' it."

I marveled at the economic system the city had spawned.

"Hop in the back," the officer said.

I opened the door for Bela and climbed in after her.

"We really appreciate this, Officer," Bela said.

"Call me Frank."

"Frank it is."

"Now Luke—it is Luke right?" He watched me in the rearview mirror. "Bela here tells me your dad is missing. Correct?"

"Correct."

"And no one has seen him since before the storm, correct?"

Bela and I both answered. "Correct."

"And he's not contacted either of you? Or any acquaintances or kin?"

I stole a look at Bela. She was staring out her window at someone walking past. "That's right, Frank." I spoke for both of us. "He's missing." I pulled the photo from my pocket and held it up.

Frank reached through the thin metal bars separating us and

quickly looked at the photo. "Hmm, nothing, but that doesn't mean much. Someone's seen him, you gotta believe that."

Officer Rostron started his cruiser and pulled out onto Canal Street. "I can get us just about anywhere we need to be. I've got an hour, ninety minutes tops."

"Where do you recommend we start?"

"Convention Center. Might be someone there who knows something. I know there are Red Cross and FEMA reps everywhere. Should be someone who knows what kinds of records were kept about who went where. Sound OK?"

I looked over at Bela. She was still looking out her window.

"Bela?" I put my hand on her arm.

"Sorry—yes, Frank, that sounds OK to me."

"Good. Done and done, sweetheart." He quickly looked over his shoulder. "Oh, for pinko's sake. I'm sorry," he said. "I say that to everyone. Didn't mean a thing by it."

"It's OK, Frank." Her voice was gentle and forgiving. "I know."

"Next stop, Morial Convention Center. It's just about a mile away."

Frank began weaving our way through the mess. I pulled my camera from my bag and attached my telephoto lens. Bela was staring out the window again.

"You all right over there?" I asked.

She waited a few seconds before turning to me. "Yeah, it's just a lot to take in."

"Right you are." I wondered how many times she and Jezebel, and Jerome too, had stopped to cry since August 29th.

I put my camera to my eye. This most routine act, something I'd done so many times the movement was involuntary, suddenly felt like sliding under a warm blanket during a Manhattan blizzard. I took a few shots of the trash. Piles of it. Mountains of it.

Are there people in those piles? I thought.

I took photos of signs—signs hanging from the tops of buildings that were covered with debris where victims had waited for a ride out of town. While waiting for some military traffic to pass at an intersection, I took a picture of a mound pushed tightly up against what looked like an office building. A sheet covered it and duct tape wrapped it tight at three places. I saw what looked like a note taped to the side. Later that night I blew that photo up on my laptop and clearly saw these words written in brown magic marker: WE'VE BEEN TAKEN TO HOUSTON. THIS IS MY MOTHER, LORI CHRISTY. SHE DIED HONORABLY. PLEASE TREAT HER THAT WAY.

I noticed that Officer Rostron saw the body, too. He crossed himself and pulled away. I decided not to point it out to Bela.

"Officer," I said, "sorry—*Frank*—what can you tell me about the night the storm hit?"

"Not much, I wasn't here yet. I got asked to come down the

next day, early afternoon. Sergeant called me and said they needed all the help they could get. It's about a six-hour drive. I got here by dark. There were police coming in from all over. I heard there's at least one officer from every state here by now, but I don't know if that's legit or not. No matter, we seem to be everywhere you look."

"So the levees had breached by the time you arrived?"

"Affirmative. The city was still filling. We—well, really the Coast Guard I guess, and some civilians—were working to rescue people from rooftops, car tops, bridges, the whole shebang. A guy I drove down here with said he rescued a guy and his parrot from a ladder. No lie. A ladder. The man was carrying it on top of his truck. When the water rushed the street, he hopped out, set the ladder in the bed of his truck—A-frame type, you know—and grabbed his parrot cage from the cab. Was standing on the ladder when my buddy came down in a flatboat. Couldn't see the top of the truck cab anymore, just this ladder sticking up. Might have saved his life that the guy painted houses for a living."

"Incredible," I said.

"So many stories like that, though. Tons of 'em. Real people became heroes. Put their lives at risk to save others." He choked on the words. "I'm sorry, I'm sorry."

"Don't be," Bela said. "You're probably due."

Frank gathered his composure as quickly as he'd lost it and

continued driving. A few blocks later he pulled over and turned off the engine.

I put my camera around my neck.

"Right over there is where Honoré helped the woman and her babies."

"Honoré?" I asked.

"Lieutenant General Honoré, the three-star. He's the guy Nagin called 'John Wayne.' He's a bad dude. Been getting stuff done and done *right*. I hear he saw a woman with her little babies and scooped them right up. She'd passed out on the street from the heat and Honoré appeared outta nowhere to save the babies. Everyone is talking about it."

"I've heard that story, too," Bela said.

"More stories like that one will surface, I'm sure of it." Frank put on his sunglasses. "So here we are. This area is really locked down tight right now. We'll walk the last block."

"Whatever you say," I offered.

Frank turned around again and looked directly at me. "This is the center of it all. You understand that?" Frank sounded very authoritative.

"Yes."

"Even if only a fraction of what we've heard about this place, about what went down here, is true, it's a miracle anyone survived. Anyone who came here to help, especially after hearing the rumors in the street, deserves a medal in my book. This was the definition of a high-risk environment."

I was pretty confident I understood the seriousness of what had occurred there.

"Ready?"

"Yep."

Frank got out and opened the back door on Bela's side. We both stepped out and onto the sidewalk. "Stay close," he said. We followed him down the street toward the Convention Center.

We passed by two dozen members of the military and National Guard.

Some had their weapons drawn.

All had some degree of fear in their wide eyes.

So many of these soldiers are kids, I thought. *Nineteen, maybe twenty years old?*

The first time we were stopped, Frank said, "They're with me."

"With me," he said the second time.

"Mine," he said the final time, gesturing to us as we passed by two guards near one of the main entrances. "Want to see inside?"

"No," Bela said immediately. "I'll wait here."

"You sure?" I asked.

"Completely."

Frank walked away, approached a contractor, gestured to us,

then pulled two white masks from a box on the ground. He returned and handed me one.

I put it on. "We'll be right back," I told Bela.

Frank put on his own mask and then placed his strong hand on my shoulder. "You want to see this?"

"I do."

"It's crazy filth and death like you've never imagined."

"Understood."

He pushed the door open and held it for me. The smell didn't wait for me to step in. Out of the corner of my eye, I saw Bela cover her nose and mouth and walk away.

"You weren't exaggerating," I said, gagging.

He said something I couldn't understand. His mouth was hidden under both his mask *and* his uniform collar.

Frank led me through the lobby. We passed hazmat workers beginning the daunting process of undoing Katrina's human consequences. A water fountain had been pulled off the wall. The metal gates covering a concession stand lay on the floor. Empty Styrofoam cups and plastic lids were tossed everywhere. Cabinet doors hung from their hinges.

Frank opened a service door, revealing a pitch-black hallway. He pulled a flashlight from the side of his belt. "Come on," he managed. "I'll show you the food-service area."

The hallway smelled even worse than the airy lobby had. Small mounds of feces and stained newspapers or magazines appeared every so often. What appeared to be dried urine was everywhere. With little warning I doubled over, pulled my mask down, and threw up in a trash can. I was thankful I couldn't see what was in it.

"Frank," I called ahead to him, wiping my mouth on my shirtsleeve. "I can't. I can't go this way. Come—" I threw up again, this time on the floor.

He turned around and led us back the way we had come. I quickly scanned the lobby again as I trotted out the door. Bela was sitting in the shade. I took my camera off my neck, collapsed near her, and put my head between my knees.

"Luke? You all right?"

I nodded but kept my head down. I saw Frank's boots approach. He said nothing.

"That bad?"

"Uh-huh."

"I'm sorry. I would have gone, but I knew I wouldn't make it."

"Uh-huh."

"You need anything?" She put her hand on the center of my back. I stayed crouched another moment.

"I'm good." After another long moment, I slowly sat up and continued breathing heavily through my mouth.

"Sorry, partner," Frank said. "I knew it would be rough; I've had to go in there a few times myself. Hasn't gotten much better. And trust me, I've thrown up too. Don't sweat it. It happens."

"Were there still bodies out in the open?" Bela asked Frank.

"Didn't see any, but we didn't get in quite that far. As of a couple days ago there were still some in the freezer. I think Command decided it was better to leave them there, safe, until they have someplace proper to take them. It's not refrigerated, mind you, but it's more decent than the street or the bathrooms."

I was breathing easier.

"I'll ask around," Frank said. "See if I can find someone who knows what's up and what's down. Stand by." He turned and walked toward a camouflaged tent.

"Are you sorry you went in?"

"No," I answered quickly and confidently. "I wanted to see it with my own eyes."

"Get any pictures?"

"Didn't need to," I said, putting my left index finger to my temple. "They're all right here."

I leaned forward again toward the ground, my palms pressed against the dead grass. Bela put one hand on top of mine and the other on my back. She applied the softest kind of pressure.

We sat quietly.

I felt a mixture of emotions impossible to have predicted.

Impossible to describe.

The smell from inside the Convention Center had coated my sinuses.

Frank returned, carrying a white slip of paper. "As expected, they don't know much here. No real records of who went where. Rumor is they did all that at the other end—at the receiving city. But they gave me a number for the Red Cross. Call this and have them check every list they've got. If your dad took a plane or a bus out of here, these guys should know where he ended up." He got down on one knee next to me and put a hand on my shoulder. "What else can I do?"

"Let's go home," Bela said.

CHAPTER
20

I don't recall much about the drive back to Verses.

I didn't stick my camera out the window, watch for unclaimed dead bodies, or gawk at the military presence. I just sat in the backseat with my head on the headrest and my eyes closed. Bela, too, was quiet.

"I still can't get over this place," Frank said absently. "It really *is* a bowl. Look over there, two blocks is all, water covers the street, but go another block and it's five, maybe ten feet deep. Then you got this dry ridge of land along the river on the south side, up to the west, too. Craziness. Here I am going down a one-way street. No lights. No stop signs. I didn't know what to expect, but in my craziest dreams I couldn't have imagined I'd have seen *this*."

Frank rambled on until we reached the club. He got out and once again opened Bela's door on the curb side of the street.

"I'm sorry you didn't see more of the city, or get to ask more people about your dad."

"I saw plenty," I said, shaking his hand. My stomach was still tight and achy.

"Anything else I can do?" Frank looked at Bela.

"No. But thank you, Frank, for trying."

"You'll try calling Houston?"

"Sure will," she answered.

He said good-bye and drove off. I doubted I'd ever forget him or what he showed me.

We walked back into the club. Quiet again. A huge stack of MREs had been added to the collection against one wall.

"I'll see who's around," Bela said as she walked back into the kitchen.

I climbed the stairs, still feeling a little queasy, and sat on my bed—the couch—in the hallway. I dialed the number Frank had given me and spent ten minutes on hold only to find out that the Red Cross didn't have a "Charles Millward" or a "Charlie Millward" or even a "C Millward" on any of their lists of New Orleans evacuees.

"Try again," the woman on the phone said. "We're still consolidating lists. Keep hope."

I thanked her, hung up, and spent some time in the bathroom brushing my teeth and washing my face. Then I sat back on the couch and powered on my camera to view the pictures I'd taken en route to the Convention Center. If the images were so powerful on a small digital preview screen, I wondered how they'd look blown up. I quickly turned off the camera to conserve power—I had no idea how long it would be until I could charge anything again—and I walked down the hallway toward the rooms I'd not seen yet.

The first room held a trumpet resting on a polishing cloth, what I recognized as two trombone cases, and enough other instruments to resemble a musical instrument ICU.

The room Tater and Hamp had entered yesterday was open enough I could see in without entering. Just inside the door a suitcase and two Wal-Mart bags appeared ready to accompany someone somewhere. There were also two piles of clothes—one clean, one dirty, I reasoned. The small pile was probably the clean one. In the middle of the floor there was a twin mattress, an air mattress, and several blankets stacked on top of one another to create a third bed. A few MREs sat atop an overflowing trash can. The whole room smelled like the lake I'd learned to swim in.

The door to the next room needed a gentle nudge to see inside. A woman was asleep under a table that held an unplugged computer, a stack of binders, and some dirty paper plates. The walls were adorned with watercolors of the Mississippi and the Bayou. Brass bands. Parades. Vibrancy. I pulled the door all the way shut and returned downstairs.

"There he is," Jezebel said as I came into view on the spiral stairs. "I understand you had a tough go." She met me at the bottom of the stairs and hugged me.

"It was something."

"I haven't even been able to go in there. Haven't had a need, really. But if it's even close to what I've heard, then no thanks, right?" She hugged me again. "I can't tell you how glad I am you came."

"Thanks, I'm really glad too." It hit me I hadn't been hugged by a woman who I hadn't been dating since my mother died.

"Jerome and Schubert are making some food out back in the crawfish boilers. Gas is still turned off, but we've got propane." She rubbed her hands vigorously up and down my back before releasing me from her comfortable embrace. "We're saying good-bye to someone tonight."

"Yeah?"

"Toby, though we just call him Castle. He's a longtime friend of the club, worked here on and off for maybe five years. His sister is dying up in Washington, D.C."

"I'm sorry." That's what you say when you hear someone is dying.

"She got evacuated right before the storm, but Castle stuck around to deal with their dogs. Find them homes before he went up to be with her."

"She was injured in Katrina?"

"No, no, she's been with cancer for years. Don't remember what kind. Doesn't matter really when the doctors tell you it's about over."

"I'm sorry," I said again.

"So we're saying good-bye to Castle tonight." This time she said it with resolve. "We've got to make something out of this food or throw it away. Oysters, jambalaya, rice, and red beans. Won't be four-star, but it could be worse. Normally places like us are all about frozen burgers, fries, pizza. College-kid cuisine, we call it."

"Can't wait." I wondered where Bela had gone.

"I bet everyone who's left in the Quarter finds us before the night is up."

Home maybe?

"You want to take a walk? It will be a while still."

I didn't, but I said yes anyway.

"Back in a while, Jerome!" she yelled loudly, very loudly, to the back. "I'm locking the door behind me!" We stepped out onto the sidewalk and she did as promised. "I worry with no one up front."

"Understood."

"You been to Jackson Square yet?"

"No, ma'am."

"I will seriously consider smacking you if you say that again."

Despite the fact she wasn't smiling, I still figured she had to be kidding. "You're joking, right?"

"Test me." Now she did smile, even bigger than last time we'd talked. "You need to relax, Luke. Loosen up."

"Loosen up? How can you say that? How can you say you're

relaxed in the middle of this?" We began to walk the two and a half blocks to Jackson Square.

I tried to ignore the rotting, wretched-smelling food the bars and restaurants had tossed into the alleys and streets.

"You heard of denial?" she asked rhetorically. "It's a beautiful drug."

Given her understanding of my father's past and what amounted to my mother's suicide, it felt like an odd choice of words. She read that, too.

"I apologize for that." She looped her arm in mine. "I only mean that I'm numb from it right now. I'm up and down. Crying one minute, laughing at fate the next. Dear, I suspect there will be plenty of time to dwell on this mess when the streets dry and the men with guns return home." As she said that, seven or eight National Guardsmen crossed in front of us.

She continued. "Luke, I've lost people in this. Good friends. People I loved. Some are dead. Some were shipped off on a bus or plane to a new city where they'll never want to leave. And I don't blame them a bit."

For the first time since I became consumed with the storm, I contemplated what it must feel like to know your neighbors might not be dead, but you still might not ever see them again.

"They might as well be," I said quietly.

"What was that?"

I shook my head. "Nothing."

We arrived at Jackson Square. Soldiers and policemen were everywhere. Protecting the gates. Smoking. Swapping rumors. Men who looked suspiciously like Secret Service agents roamed the grounds inside the gates and by the church that overlooked the square.

"That's St. Louis Cathedral," she said, pointing to it. "On the opposite end is the Moon Walk overlooking the river."

"Boardwalk?"

"*Moon Walk.* It was named for the mayor back then—Moon Landrieu."

"Interesting. Related to the senator?"

"Mary's his daughter. Rumor has it his son, Mitch, might run for mayor," she said as we continued walking the perimeter.

I tried to appreciate two hundred fifty years of blended Spanish and French architecture fighting for its life amidst Mother Nature's war zone.

"During my time I've seen it all here. Painters. Musicians. Some greats have played here for tips, in fact. This was *the* place when I was growing up. Our mother would bring us down on the weekends. What she didn't know was that Jerome and me would sometimes come down by ourselves after school. Jerome learned to play the trumpet down here."

"Neat."

"You know who else got his start down here?"

"Harry Connick, Jr."

"Maybe. But that's not where I was going with that. Try Charlie Millward. Started right here."

"His start?"

"I'm not saying he learned to *play* here, but this is where he started in New Awlins. Came down here and played jazz, blues, some folk, worked on that song of his constantly."

A pair of policemen in T-shirts and carrying guns on their backs stopped us. One had a crew cut; one had no hair at all. The bald one spoke. "You two deaf?"

"Excuse me?" Jezebel said with all the attitude I would have expected.

"Are you *deaf?*" the bald one repeated.

"Not yet, but if you keep yelling at me I just might be."

"Aren't we a yippy little thing—"

"What's the matter, officer?" I jumped in.

"There's something called a mandatory evacuation order in effect. Heard of that? Mandatory? You two need a dictionary?"

"Oh, now *listen*—" Before Jez could finish that thought, I'd pulled her behind me.

"We're working recovery, sir."

"Recovery? Really? Cause you look like you're on a lover's stroll."

His crew-cut comrade laughed.

"We're Coast Guard Auxiliary," I said.

"Yeah?"

"That's right. We're taking some downtime. A few minutes, that's it."

"Is that all right with you, Kojak?" Jez just couldn't help herself.

I stepped in front of her again. "She's tired. We're all beat, right?"

"Whatever. Just stay out of the way."

"Thank you. We will." I remembered Dad's photo. "Wait, officer." I held the photo up. "Have you seen this man?"

They both looked it over.

"Nope," they said one after another and walked away. Ten steps later Kojak looked over his shoulder and launched a string of mostly unrecognizable gibberish. But the words "jungle fever" were clear as day.

"Pigs," Jezebel said as we watched them engage another man on the other side of St. Ann Street.

"Some are better than others."

"And some share more DNA with farm animals than others."

"Touché," I conceded. "Actually I always remind myself there are unkind, unethical, untoward people in *every* line of work. And sometimes otherwise good people have very bad days. Makes me feel better when I run across someone like that."

"Your dad teach you that?"

I made eye contact. "I honestly don't remember."

She sighed and slid her arm through mine again. "Let's walk."

The sight must have bewildered more than just Kojak and his partner: a thirty-something white male walking arm-in-arm with a fifty-something black woman in the aftermath of the worst natural disaster in U.S. history. Never mind the fact she was supposed to have been my stepmother.

As we walked I wondered if this would be the one memory of the trip that I might recall with affection in my old age.

We turned left on Dumaine and walked north toward Louis Armstrong Park.

"So tell me what you *do* remember."

"Come again?" I knew what she'd said.

"Charlie. What do you remember about Charlie?"

"Jez, it's not like he's been dead since I was a kid. I remember plenty."

"Fine. What's the last thing you remember?"

"A phone call from Texas. Broke. Drunk. And, forgive me, I know you loved him, but pathetic."

"Tell me about the call."

I did, reluctantly.

Jez didn't look at me for three blocks.

We walked the rest of the way to the park in silence. More soldiers and police officers. Volunteers at a Red Cross truck were handing out Styrofoam containers of food to relief workers.

Trees were cut in half, like Goliath had snapped them in two.

Against one tree I noticed a body covered by trash bags that were held down by rocks at the corners. A pair of feet in brown tube socks poked out into the sun and a pair of broken flip-flops sat at the body's side.

A trade?

Jez nodded to the west and we walked down North Rampart. We passed Louis Armstrong Park and Congo Square. The place where jazz was born couldn't have been more quiet.

"See that place?" Jez pointed to a souvenir shop.

"Uh-huh."

"Your dad knew the guy who used to own that place. I forget his real name since everyone just called him Olson."

"And . . ."

"And they were good friends."

I nodded and we continued walking.

"He was from around here somewhere," Jez continued, "but his wife was from California. Little place called Ferndale."

"If you say so," I said. We were a full block away from the souvenir shop now.

"Ever see the movie *The Majestic?*"

"With Jim Carrey, right?"

"That's it."

"Yeah, pretty good movie."

"It was filmed in Ferndale."

"Hmm." I wasn't entirely sure how interested I was supposed to be.

"Olson and his wife used to work together every day at the shop, close as could be. Then one day they argued about something—who knows what—and they never stopped."

"Arguing?"

"That's right. It's like they woke up one morning and realized they didn't like each other anymore."

"That's too bad."

"Let's cross here." Jez put her arm in mine again and we walked from one dirty sidewalk across the street to another.

"One day she said she wasn't feeling well and wasn't coming down to the store." Jez's story persisted. "So Olson goes alone, works all day, comes home, and she's gone. Left a note saying she was going home to Ferndale."

"Wow."

"That's right—wow."

"Definitely sad," I added, "but not uncommon anymore, unfortunately."

Jez squeezed my arm a little tighter. "Olson came by the club looking for your dad. They talked all night. Then Charlie spent a couple days at the store, helping out. Wouldn't take any money, either. By the end of the third day, maybe the fourth, your dad sat Olson down and handed him a plane ticket."

"California," I predicted.

"That's right. Your father, that sweet, sweet man, convinced

Olson he had no choice but go to little ol' Ferndale and fight for his wife, fall for her, help her fall in love all over again."

"Did they?"

"Sure did. And your dad worked the shop while he was gone. I helped out a little of course."

"And they came back to the city?"

"Nope. Those two didn't just fall in love with each other, Olson fell in love with that town. They sold the shop here and bought a little motel and general store out there. Best hot dog in the west, Olson said. Never happier."

"Nice ending."

"That it is. And Charlie Millward's going to heaven for endings like that."

We'll see, I thought.

We walked a block or two in silence.

Jez turned her head to me. "Tell me about Las Vegas."

"You've never been?"

"Heavens, boy, that's not what I meant. Tell me about your *dad* in Vegas."

"Oh. See Charles Millward *was* Vegas. Even Bugsy didn't love that town as much as my father did."

She shook her head in disapproval without bothering to turn toward me. "Why did he love it?"

"I don't know. The thrill. The money." I looked at Jez, her gaze fixed on the horizon ahead.

"Maybe it made him feel better about himself?"

"This was not a man with a self-esteem problem. He had it all until Mom died."

"Go on," Jez prodded.

I sighed. Noticeably. "I guess it started in Nashville. After I left home, he moved there to play music, hoping to hit it big, I guess. We spoke pretty often for a while. He was in and out of programs for the drinking, though still denying he was a true alcoholic."

I rewound.

"I suppose I've always known it started with his poker club at home. Mom was sick, sleeping all the time, sad, angry, refusing to deal with her own mother's accident—the whole package for clinical depression. Of course I didn't know much about it then. And I wanted to believe Dad. We thought she'd pull through."

I looked at Jez and stopped walking.

She stopped, too, and turned to face me.

"Is it weird? Me talking about my mother?"

She smiled exactly like my mother would have before the pills. "Not at all."

"Dad played cards at home to get through it. I never asked him this, but I think he justified it in his mind by saying he was close to her. The cards and the guys and the excitement were fine because he was near enough to help when she needed it. But the cards just became an excuse to drink. Even as a kid I could see that."

"That's called a coping mechanism," Jez said. "I know. I'm using one or two or seven of my own right now. So are you."

"OK, fine, I see that. But then Mom dies, I go off to school, Dad sells the house and goes to Nashville, does his thing, blows through most of what he made on the house—at least what was left after he sent me a chunk of it—and the next thing I know, he calls from Vegas."

"The weekend you graduated from college."

"That's right. Graduation. He calls from a hotel room downtown. The Nugget I think. He's out of money. Bone dry. Needs help."

"And you gave it."

"Well, sure I did. I lived on a budget during college so I had some cash stowed away." I paused, remembering. "I thought that was it. I thought he was seriously going to give up booze and turn his life around. Now I'm convinced if he hadn't run out of money, he would have won himself a gambling problem to go with the bottle."

"And . . ."

"With all due respect, Jezebel, why am I telling you a story you already know the ending to?" No use hiding my irritation with someone as perceptive as Jezebel.

"Because I don't think we agree on the ending, Luke."

"Oh, please."

"Luke, we don't get to decide how many chances a man gets to recover. He gets as many as it takes. Your dad needed one more in New Awlins, and he got it. And thank the Lord he did."

I turned my back on her and began walking toward Bourbon Street.

"Every time you rip your father, you're ripping me. Do you get that? You're making a judgment on *my* judgment."

I stopped.

"That's reading too much, Jez."

"Is it? You think I fall for every drunk fool who walks into my club? That's what he was to you, right? You think I just throw myself at a shaggy white man because that's the best I can do?"

"Don't." I stepped forward and pointed. "Don't tell me that after six exotic months with Dad—or whatever it was—that you knew him better than I did. I know how needy he could be. But I also know he needed to *save* people. One or the other, never in the middle. Mom. Coworkers. Neighbors. It made him feel better about himself."

"And you think I needed saving when I met your father?"

"I don't know. But I see what you're doing. I see it. And I think I know my father better than just another girlfriend would."

No words could have cut her more.

CHAPTER
21

Alone.

There was no good reason for it. The streets had policemen wandering in and out of the huge tents on Canal. The two to three hundred residents of the Quarter who remained scampered to and from buildings around me. I was a ten-minute walk from people who didn't know me, but who managed to care anyway.

I shook a random, vivid image of the Convention Center from my mind.

I began retracing my steps to Jackson Square and tried calling Jordan. Nothing. I tried again, and again. Nothing. I sent a text message.

J, CALL ME

There was no way of knowing whether it went through.

Then my phone rang.

FOUNTAIN REALTY

"Hello?"

"Luke. Hi! How's it going?"

"OK. You got my text message?"

"Yeah, of course." Her voice was comforting. "Texts might be more reliable. Let's try that for now."

A police officer ran to a man who was on the ground ahead of me on the same block. "Carlisle! Get over here!" Another officer sprinted across the street. They knelt beside the man and administered CPR.

I stopped a few feet away and watched.

"You there? Everything OK, Luke?" The phone was still by my ear.

One officer gave the man chest compressions, the other mouth-to-mouth. "Come on!" He grunted the words. "Come on!" The other checked for a pulse, then put his ear by the man's mouth. Others had gathered to watch.

"Come on, buddy. Come on," I said quietly.

"Luke?" Jordan said again.

The CPR continued for several cycles. Eventually a third officer spoke up. "He's gone."

They're not supposed to die after the storm, I thought. *How many others will die and never be counted as Katrina's victims?*

They looked for the man's ID. Nothing. One of the policemen picked up the man's limp body and carried it across the street to a patch of grass. He crossed himself, mouthed a prayer, and covered the dead man's face with a handkerchief he had pulled from his pocket.

"Luke? Luke?"

"Sorry, Jordan. I'm here." I began walking again, stepping around the place where the man had collapsed and died.

"What's happening?"

"Nothing," I said. "Just . . . it's nothing. The streets are chaotic."

"How was your day? Any progress finding your dad?"

"Not really. We saw the Convention Center."

"Inside?"

"Yeah."

"Bad?"

"Yeah."

"You want to talk about it?"

"Not really." The smell filled my nose again.

"What about your dad?"

"Nothing."

"Nothing at all? What are they saying? How the heck can they just *lose* him?"

"It's not that easy, Jordan. People are missing all over the city, all over the entire Gulf. Thousands of people. Dad's just one guy who nobody knows."

"What about Houston? The dome—what's it called? Was he taken there?"

"No one knows yet. I tried some special Red Cross hotline today, but they didn't have Dad's name on any list."

"You've been showing the photo around, though, right?"

I realized I hadn't, but saying yes felt better.

Her silence on the other end meant she was planning. "Let me help."

"You're not coming down here."

"Why not? I could leave in the morning and be there in two days."

"Jordy, what's happened here is something I can't describe. Even the photos don't tell the story well enough. Just trust me. It's not safe. They're pushing people out, not letting them in."

"So give me something to do."

"Like what?"

"Like make calls. Send e-mails. Faxes. Visits to the White House. Whatever. I'll do whatever I can."

We agreed that her having a reliable landline and Internet access was useful. I told her to get a key from the maintenance man in my building and find a picture of my father from my apartment to scan and post online. She would visit the chat rooms, message boards, Red Cross, and FEMA resources.

"Spread the picture far and wide, talk to anyone and everyone," I said. I also agreed she should try calling Houston.

She promised to call or text with news. "I'm sorry I'm not there."

"I know. Me too."

By the time we'd hung up I was back at Jackson Square. I watched even more men, and now a few women as well, who looked like spies roaming the grounds.

A few days later I learned the president would speak from that very spot.

I stopped two men in FEMA baseball caps. "Excuse me, have you seen this man?"

"Are you kidding?" one of them answered.

"Of course not."

"We just ushered an entire city east, west, and north. Think we'd remember *one* man?"

"It's my father."

They both looked down.

"I'm sorry," the other man said, shaking my hand. "We haven't."

I gave them a "thanks, anyway" and sat on a bench. I pretended to hear music from the park. Trumpets, bucket drummers, open cases and upturned hats filling with silver, a man on a saxophone.

A man on a saxophone with whiskey on his breath.

A man on a saxophone with whiskey on his breath and a broken heart.

CHAPTER
22

It was easy to lose track of time.

The sun had almost set but the temperature still had to be in the high eighties. My armpits were sweaty, and my shirt was glued to my back like Saran wrap on the top of Mom's three-bean casserole.

I stood up and pulled my shirt away from my skin. I'd have paid any price for a shower.

I'm starving.

The walk back to Verses was short and dreadful. I hoped Bela was around. I really hoped Jez hadn't told anyone what a foolish heel I'd been.

The door was open. "You're late, son." Jerome saw me first.

"For what?"

"Food. You hungry?"

My stomach growled loudly.

"Thought so. Go through the kitchen and outside. On the

patio back there there's plenty of cooked rice and fish. Cooked enough fish to feed *twice* as many as Jesus fed. No loaves though. No ice either." He chuckled to himself. "Jesus, you know I love that story." By then he was talking to himself—or to Jesus— because I was almost to the kitchen door.

A man and a woman I hadn't seen before whispered as I walked by and smiled politely as if we were passing in a hallway at the doctor's office. I nodded a silent hello.

Jez, Bela, and a man I hadn't met yet were shoving trash in a bag.

Only the man looked up. He was about my height, a touch taller, maybe an even six feet. He had brown skin, and at best, a quarter-inch of black hair on his head. Athletic. He wore cut-off sweats and a tight undershirt with stains I suspected were food, blood, and vomit. If he had more than four-percent body fat he was hiding it very well.

The man approached me with such eagerness I thought he might punch me in the face.

Please shake my hand, I thought.

He did. And then he gave me a man-hug. "We didn't think you were coming."

"I've been getting that a lot."

"I bet you have. But seriously, good to meet you, dude."

We haven't met.

"You *are* Charlie's kid, right?"

"I am." As I answered, I watched Bela climb into the back of a van parked in the alley. And either Jez *had* gone deaf since her encounter with Officer Baldy or she was ignoring us as she made use of every inch of her Glad bag.

"I'm Toby Castle. Call me Castle."

The man with the dying sister.

"Good to meet you, Castle. I'm sorry about your sister."

He looked at Jez then back at me. "Good thing none of us have secrets, huh?"

I didn't feel like it but I smiled anyway. Bela climbed out of the van with a cardboard carton of something and walked through the back door to the kitchen. Jez followed.

"Don't worry, dude. She's cool."

"Cool? She looks like she doesn't recognize me."

"That's Jez. It passes—you just got to get in her face and apologize."

I know.

"She's having a ridiculously hard time right now. What with all the worrying about your old man." He mashed down the trash even farther and tied the top of the bag. "I bet there aren't but three people worrying about trash in this city right now." He pulled another bag from a box on the ground. "Feels normal, cleaning up after our own mess, know what I mean?"

"More than ever."

"I wonder what it will look like when I get back. My sister, as

Jez already told you, is hanging tight at a hospital up in D.C. A friend from the other side of the lake is driving me up tomorrow morning, crack of dawn." He opened the trash bag. "Could you grab those empty rice bags?"

I walked to one of the boilers, picked up an armful of plastic bags, and pushed them to the bottom of the bag he held wide open.

"So, so, so, what *will* my city look like when I get back? That's the hundred-billion-dollar question. Isn't that what they're saying it's costing? Will it be the same? Will the people come back—that's the real kicker, isn't it? The other cities can keep the scum. We don't need back the felons and haters, the complainers, the cradle-to-gravers. Give us back our teachers, our doctors, our business people, our good-hearted blacks, whites, yellows, purples, and whatever-elsers." He took a much-needed breath. "Uh-huh, Toby Castle wants back his hard-working-get-your-hands-dirty-and-make-a-difference people."

This guy needs a congregation and a radio show, too.

"And that, Luke, is my message of the day."

"So what about you? Are *you* coming back?"

"Ha! Love your style, dude. Love it! *Yes,* this proud black man is coming back to make it better than ever. No doubt about it. None. No shred. This is my home."

"New Orlins?" I tried.

"Not bad!" He laughed. "Pound that." He put his clenched fist up and I tapped it with mine. "Not bad at all."

We made more small talk while scouring the patio and alley for whatever trash we were willing to touch with our bare hands.

"You knew my father well?" I asked.

"Pretty dag-on well, considering he hadn't been in the city but a year."

"Six months, I'm told."

"Dang, that's it? Got to know that crazy man—no offense—pretty well then. Feels like I've known him much longer. Good man."

We tied up another bag and put it with the first one against the wall at the back of the building.

"Mind if I ask what you know about me?" I asked.

"Not as much as you probably think, or as much as Jez does. Your old man—that bother you if I call him that?"

I shook my head.

"Your old man didn't talk to anyone like he talked to Jez. Haven't ever seen two people hit it off and fall like those two. Not ever. Dude, they were in some serious love."

"Seems like it."

"Your dad and me spent time together doing the clinics, working on that song of his, but didn't talk much at the club. Just no time. Doesn't look it now, but this is a fixture in the Quarter. Sandwiches, wings, booze, and music every night. *Live* music. A lot of places use DJs. Verses has always been about red-hot live music."

Castle opened the back of the van and sat on the bumper.

I joined him. "You said clinics. What's that?"

"Dude, my bad." He slapped his chest. "I forgot you haven't talked to your dad in forever."

Two years—let's not exaggerate.

"What's that called? Estranged?"

I now prefer to think we were on a break. "Something like that."

"Your dad came in one day and sat down the owner—that's Mr. Hunt, but he's not around much—and Jerome and Jez. Charlie said he'd been down at Jackson Square talking to some kids who were hanging out by the musicians. You know folks play for tips down there all the time."

"Uh-huh."

"Charlie asked the kids if they wanted to learn how to play, too. And of course they did. He ran back here, got his sax, and spent half the dag-on day down there teaching those kids."

"So that's a clinic."

"No, that's a jam session." Castle laughed and rubbed his head. "He told us all about it and said he wanted to sponsor some clinics."

"Sponsor?"

"Verses really did the sponsoring, but your dad ran the joint.

Roped me into going around with him. Schools, Boys and Girls Clubs, YMCA—wherever your dad could get us in."

"Wow."

"You know it. All that and he'd come back here and jam at night with the band." He hopped off the bumper. "That's where Jesse came from."

He answered my next question before I could get my mouth open.

"The van—Jesse. Mr. Hunt loved your dad's clinics. Thought it was good for the kids, good for your dad, and he was man enough to admit it, good for the club, too. Big old fifteen-passenger van rolling around town with Verses splashed across both sides."

I wasn't sure how long Jez had been standing there, but when I hopped off the bumper and walked around the side of the van, she was leaning against the doorjamb with her arms folded.

"I'm out," Castle said, but this time gave me a two-armed hug. "I got a couple people to say good-bye to."

"Be careful," Jez said as he kissed her on the cheek. "The guys with guns are grouchy out there today."

I pulled my phone from my pocket and checked for a signal. I thought it showed five bars, but I wasn't really paying attention.

Jez was. "You waiting for someone?"

I flipped the phone shut and dropped it back in my pocket. "No."

Jez stared at me with her arms crossed. She'd been crying—again.

"I didn't mean it," I said to the ground.

Nothing.

"I'm a fish out of water here." *Oh, my.* "That's not at all what I meant."

She still wasn't smiling.

"I'm sorry, Jez. I am really sorry."

Nothing.

"I'm sorry for saying what I did. I know you were more than a girlfriend. You were engaged. I know. I'm sorry. You're obviously different from anyone my dad ever met. What am I saying? I don't even know if there *were* any other women between my mother and you."

Nothing.

"You going to let me off the hook or what?"

Jez laughed and finally uncrossed her arms. She moved to me and wrapped them around my shoulders.

"How many bad puns was that?"

"Too many."

"I apologize, Jez. Forgive me?"

"Of course. That's what family does."

Bela appeared, gliding through the doorway.

Jez couldn't see her.

I sure could.

"You two done?" Bela asked. "I've got one plate of food left but it's cooling fast."

"I'm famished."

"Get in there, then. There's rice and beans and I bet enough fish you won't ever want to eat it again."

I didn't care for fish anyway, but I'd have eaten a whale if Bela had put it in front of me.

Bela gestured for me to step past her through the doorway and into the kitchen. I walked close enough by her to think she was the only human being I'd encountered in thirty-six hours who didn't smell putrid. For more reasons than one I felt guilty for noticing.

A plate of food was in front of the barstool that was beginning to feel like it belonged to me. The food smelled magnificent and I almost had to catch the saliva from my lower lip.

In my peripheral vision I saw Jez slide a bottle of water the length of the bar. "Drink up."

I caught it without looking.

"Smooth," Bela said. She was standing across from me like a barkeep.

Jez came over and hugged me from the side. "You're a good boy, Luke." She let go and opened the front door. "I'm off to see what trouble I can find, or help to give. Back before dark." She shut the door behind her.

"She doesn't mean to treat you like a kid."

"Huh?"

She had to repeat it because I'd just taken my first bite of jambalaya—ever.

"This is even better than it smells. How is that possible?"

"It's not exactly a new recipe," she quipped.

"I know. It's just . . . there's no power, at least not right now, no fridges, no clean water. How can you cook something like this?" I put a bite so big in my mouth that had my mother been present, she would have gently reprimanded me.

"We've had power more often than you might realize, though the gossip outside is they're cutting it off indefinitely while they fix the gas lines. And ice has come a few times. Most of what's on your plate came from my people in the Quarter who left."

"Before or after?" I opened my water and took a drink.

"Both. If there's anything I've learned about living in this city, it's that people don't like wasting food. The Monday after the storm, we fried up so many hamburgers from the deep freezer— couple hundred, easy. French fries, too. The block was pretty full. Other people had stuff cooking outside, too. Smoke filled up the streets. Weren't many relief workers here yet, so it felt like just another day of Mardi Gras. Then came the rumors about the levees."

I took another drink. "Have all the days been this long?"

"How so?"

"Since the storm, have the days dragged? I feel like I've been up for three days and it's only dinnertime. I feel like I've been hit by a truck." I put the last bite of rice in my mouth and chewed slowly.

Bela took my plate. "Done?"

"And then some. Thank you."

"You're welcome." She stacked the plate with some others and wiped down the bar where I'd eaten as if it were the most normal thing in the world. "You look at any pictures from today yet?"

"Just on my camera. Some powerful shots."

"Mind if I see?"

"Really?"

"Photography has always been a hobby, but school's had to come first."

"Very cool. Come up and I'll download them on my laptop."

Bela followed me up the stairs and we settled into the soft cushions together. I set my computer on my lap and powered it up. I dug in my bag for my USB cable and attached my camera. iPhoto launched automatically and began importing the newest pictures.

"Mac guy, huh?"

"Always."

"My friends, a lot of them anyway, have them for school. I always thought they were for creative types."

"They are." I smiled. "And for future social workers."

"One day—when I win the lottery."

"Here we go," I said. "They're up."

Bela slid over to my side of the couch and leaned in to me.

"I didn't take as many today as I thought." I scrolled through the frames one-by-one, clicking quickly through the morbid photos I was almost ashamed to have taken. I didn't stop at all on the picture of the funeral taken the day before. "Sorry," I offered.

"You're a professional photographer," she said. "I understand."

We viewed all the photos I'd taken since leaving Manhattan. "That's a classic," she said of the sign I'd seen on the edge of New Orleans: STILL NO FUEL. RIDE A BIKE.

"Can I see more?" Bela asked.

"Of course." I opened the second most recent album, the pictures from Ground Zero I'd taken just days before my trip to Verses began.

"You knew them?" she asked, pointing to the Indian couple.

"No. Good people though." I took a moment to privately admire my own work. The photo of the couple walking away from the camera was strong.

"How about happier times." I opened an album labeled "Machu Picchu."

"Is that Peru?"

"It is. It's Machu Picchu."

"I have *always* wanted to go there. What a place, right?"

I enlarged a photo taken from the ancient guard shack

overlooking the ruins. Even after viewing the photos over and over, the images of the ancient Incan city astounded me.

"Look at these peaks—there are two of them, Machu Picchu, that means 'Old Mountain,' and Huayna Picchu, or 'Young Mountain.' There are these single buildings, see here."

She leaned in closer.

"You have these right next to terraces and plazas. A lot of these were homes. Most of the buildings are residences made from white granite. The stones are just enormous, and no one is quite sure how the Incas moved them and put them in place. Other buildings—hold on, let me find a better photo. . . . See, these were actually carved into the bedrock. It's miraculous. They made something out of nothing up there."

I pulled up a photo of myself atop Huayna Picchu, the mountain that so many tourists climb to overlook the ruins and the Incan trail.

"You went with someone?"

"No, solo."

"Who took this?"

"A girl I met at the top of the mountain. A med student from Kansas, I think. I honestly don't recall."

More pictures.

A man and an alpaca eating opposite ends of the same piece of straw.

Another alpaca, this one looking like Bob Marley and almost smiling at my camera.

A Peruvian man along the side of the road, weaving a red-and-yellow blanket.

Two young girls in the most richly-colored dresses I'd ever seen. They posed with their llama. I'd given them each a dollar.

Finally, one of my favorites. A photo of me and a man I'd never forget, Valentine. He sold artwork outside my hotel in Cuzco and harassed me every day of my trip until I bought a painting.

I moved from Machu Picchu to black-and-white shots of my apartment. A photo of Jordan sitting at my desk with her feet propped up didn't stay on my screen long.

"Girlfriend?"

"Friend who's a girl."

"Hmm. She's pretty."

So are you, I thought. "She's a good friend. Maybe the best I've had since grade school. Plus I've known her for years so we're comfortable."

I changed the subject with pictures of Bangkok and Vertigo, one of the highest open-air bars and restaurants in the world. "That's on the sixty-first floor. We ate dinner up there. No roof, almost no rails, fantastic view."

Practically right in my ear Bela made sounds and said things that indicated she was *very* impressed.

I liked that.

"Ooooh . . . Those girls were soooo adorable . . . Wow, look at that . . . That was sweet of you . . . You *ate* up there? Not me . . ."

For almost an hour I'd completely forgotten why I'd come to New Awlins.

My cell phone reminded me.

Fountain Realty

Always punctual.

"Get that. I've got to take off and say good-bye to Castle anyway."

I flipped open the phone. "Hang on, J." I covered the mouthpiece and looked up at Bela.

"You need me to walk you home?"

"I'll be OK."

"You sure? I don't want Jerome on my case later."

"It's fine. There are still people around downstairs; I'll find someone to walk me."

"All right then. Thanks for listening."

"Thanks for talking," Bela answered. "It was fun, given the circumstances." She pointed to my camera. "You're talented, Luke Millward."

"Thanks, really, that means a lot."

"And buy me one of those some day, would you?" She pointed to my laptop with one hand and slapped my knee with the other as she crossed in front of me and disappeared down the spiral stairs. I waited until I heard conversation from the first floor.

"Hey, Jordan."

"Hey, bud."

"You get into my place OK?"

"Without a wrinkle. The picture of you two is up and every-where."

"Thanks. I hate to ask you to do all this." I couldn't have meant it more.

"Stop it. This is what I'm here for. I'd do this for you—and more—even if we weren't friends."

"Really?"

"Really. Listen to me, you're going to figure this out. I know it. I have faith in you, Luke. I *believe* in you."

"Thanks, Jordan." I had to admit the woman always knew exactly what to say.

"And I miss you."

CHAPTER

23

I dreamt someone was shaking me.

"Luke, get up, son."

Someone *was* shaking me.

"We got us a boat."

I sat up and rubbed sleep and surprise from my eyes. Jerome was standing over me.

"What time is it?" I asked.

"Six."

"Where are we going?"

"Your dad's place."

"What?"

"The five-four. Let's go, son. Get up. We're waitin' on the street."

I sat up and pulled my shoes out from under the end of the couch. I used the bathroom, splashed water on my face, matted down my hair, and ran back down the hallway and down the stairs.

"Camera," I said and scurried back up. I put it in its bag and slung it over my shoulder.

"Good morning," Jez greeted me when I walked out of the club and onto the street. Jerome stood next to her. Tater and Hamp were talking to Officer Rostron. Four others I'd seen at the club but not met yet stood to the side and talked quietly. It felt like it was seventy-five degrees already.

"Morning there."

"Hey, Frank," I answered, curious that he was there but too numb and tired to ask.

"Jerome tell you?" Jez approached me. She was wearing the same clothes she'd worn the day before. But then so were the rest of us. "We're going to your dad's place. Frank found us a flat-bottom boat not spoken for, and Tater and Hamp know some of the Coast Guard and FEMA guys at a staging area on Rampart and Elysian Fields."

It suddenly hit me. "You haven't checked Dad's place yet?"

"Yes, they did," Jez answered. "Early Monday morning, before the levees broke. The house was empty."

"You haven't gone back?" *Incredible.*

"Lots of people have been by, Luke, but the house has been empty. Sweetheart, there are still people down there, people who might still know something. That's why we're going." She looked at Jerome. "Plus we thought you might want to see his place. Maybe take whatever's dry."

It was a morbid and entirely rational suggestion.

"So it is possible my father is inside that house?"

Jerome hesitated. "No, son."

Something is telling me otherwise, I thought.

"And this is OK," I asked, "that we get in a boat and do this on our own?"

"It is if I'm in tow," Frank said. "I'll get you launched."

I didn't doubt that. His telephone-pole biceps were on full display under his painted-on blue T-shirt.

"Morning, Bela," Jez said, looking past me.

I turned around.

Bela wore a tan tank top and blue nylon basketball shorts. Her hair was back in a ponytail, tucked under a Tulane baseball cap. Her hat looked wet around the sides where it fit snugly. When she turned, I saw that a stream of water had dripped its way from her ponytail halfway down her back.

"Good morning, Jez," Bela answered. She seemed to smile a "good morning" to me, too.

I smiled a "good morning" back.

"How'd you sleep?" Jez asked.

"I didn't. Hallie is the only one left in the apartment, and she's finally leaving to meet her parents up north. We talked all night."

Before Jez could respond, Jerome raised a hand in the air. "All right, you see these people 'round you, son?" He referred to them but looked straight at me. "These people are here for you, today. Let's see what we can find. Let's find some hope."

"That's right," Jez chimed.

"'Course you know me, Jez, Bela, Tater, and Hamp. Tha's Joe Call and his girl, Cherie." He motioned to the four bystanders. "The tall guy is Baldwin, and I don't know the other one. They're friends of Castle."

They all waved or nodded. The man Jerome didn't know shook my hand and whispered, "Chuck."

"Luke, all these people have lost someone. Every one of 'em knows someone who's dead this mornin'."

Do I say thank you? I thought. *Or I'm sorry?*

I said neither, asking instead if we could take a photo.

"A what?" Jerome asked though he'd obviously heard me. He was checking his shirt for stains. There were a lot.

"A photo. I'm a photographer; this is how I record life." That wasn't the first time I'd used that phrase.

"Well, get it over with."

"I'll snap it," Frank offered.

I gave him a ten-second tutorial, and we gathered in a gangly semicircle. Jez stood at one end, next to me, and Bela, by chance, stood on the other side. The rest fanned out to her right.

I was grateful Frank didn't ask us to say "cheese."

"One, two, three." Click. "You want to check it?"

"I'm sure it's fine," I said, taking the camera from him. I

viewed the image before it disappeared into my camera's memory. It was more than fine, it was outstanding.

"Thanks, Frank."

Jerome took over again. "Let us pray."

We gathered in a circle in the middle of the street and held hands. I stood between Bela and Jez.

"Dear Lord," Jerome began. "We love Thee. We thank Thee, dear Lord, for the blessing of this day. We thank Thee, Lord, for our friend and brother Toby Castle. Get him safe to D.C., O Lord, and let his sister live until he stands by her side. Or longer, Almighty Lord above, if it is Thy will that she be healed. And Lord, we thank Thee for Luke and his mission here in New Awlins. Let us find what he is looking for, Lord."

Jez and Bela both squeezed my hands.

"And Lord, let us be safe while we look. Bless *all* those still missin', Lord, and bless all those still lookin'." He paused and finished thoughtfully. "Forgive us, Lord. Forgive us all of our trespasses. Forgive what we do today. Forgive what we do *every day.*"

There wasn't much I could imagine anyone in that circle needing to be forgiven of.

"Amen, Lord."

"Amen," we repeated.

"We're goin'. Frank will drive a few of us in his cruiser. I'll take the rest in Jesse."

Frank opened the passenger's door for me and I climbed in. Jez and Bela shared the backseat.

We sat quietly while Jerome and the others walked through the alley and loaded up in Verses' fifteen-passenger van. As soon as the nose of the van appeared in the alley, Frank pulled out and rolled around the corner onto Toulouse. We took the road north, away from the river, toward Rampart, then turned east. Rampart became St. Claude and, three blocks later, Frank parked us on the side of the road behind a dozen trucks with empty trailers and law enforcement and EMT vehicles of every conceivable make and model.

Jerome parked Jesse right behind us.

"We're here," Frank said.

I opened my door and watched a crew step onto a boat in a foot of water and begin paddling east.

"You OK?" Bela said, putting her hand on my arm.

"Mm-hmm."

Frank found a man standing by a long johnboat hitched to a trailer. The trailer's wheels kissed the edge of the water. I watched intently as Frank shook the man's hand and pointed to us.

Then he handed him three packs of cigarettes.

A moment later, he flagged us over.

Frank and Jerome pulled the boat into the water and guided it clear of the trailer. The boat didn't seem big enough to warrant a name, but along its side the owner had spelled PANGLE in mailbox-style adhesive letters. I quickly snapped a photo.

Jez and Bela boarded first, then Jerome, Tater, and Hamp. When it became clear we wouldn't all fit on the three benches, two of Castle's friends volunteered to stay behind. "We'll find somewhere else to help."

I gave both Baldwin and Chuck a man-hug. "Thanks. Thanks for being willing."

Frank shook my hand next. "Good luck, kid."

He got a man-hug, too. "Thanks, Frank."

I boarded PANGLE and Frank pushed it with his foot. Tater started the outboard motor and began navigating toward deeper water.

Frank lifted his hand in farewell.

I never saw him again.

CHAPTER
24

The plastic ball had a grinning Dora the Explorer on its side.

We floated right by it. The urge to pick it up and try to find its owner was irresistible. I scooped it up and forced it under my seat. But I never found a child to give it to.

Jez smiled.

Bela handed me hand sanitizer.

"I've got gloves in my bag for everybody," Tater said from the front of the boat.

The water was a floating yard sale with items no one wanted anymore.

Plastic lawn chairs, a yellow-and-blue Connect Four game, an Allstate Frisbee, tires for bikes, and tires for cars. Broken Big Wheels. An empty Mountain Dew bottle, an open *Pirates of the Caribbean* DVD case. A 5x7 picture of a gorgeous, smiling black girl cradling her infant brother who was wrapped in a blue blanket, crying.

I picked that up, too.

Bela gave me more hand sanitizer.

I asked Tater for a pair of gloves.

The others asked as well.

Jerome pointed out landmarks as we floated through the streets in water that ranged from a few feet to ten, judging by the waterlines on front doors.

"They say Marshall Faulk grew up right there." Jerome pointed to his left.

"The football player?"

"Uh-huh."

We passed a series of houses, maybe a full block long of them, that all had orange Xs on the doors with writing in each of the four sections of the letter.

"Slow down a little, Tater," Hamp said. "See that one? When they leave a house, they paint an X to say it's been searched. At the top of the X they put the date; in the right section, the right part of the X, they put the unit that did the search. On the left you see what danger they found to warn others—gas lines, stuff like that. At the bottom, they put the number of bodies."

The X we were looking at had a four.

We moved from the tragic orange X to one of the most striking images from all the coverage I'd seen before leaving New York:

a barge in the Lower Ninth—flooded houses all around it, crushed houses under it, missing houses in its path from the Industrial Canal. The nose of a school bus was visible right against the barge, as if the driver had parked it there.

"It's like a disaster movie," I heard Bela say into the wind behind me. I turned around in my seat in the middle of the boat and saw Jez put her arm around her.

I took a dozen photos, including one of Joe and Cherie. They shared a bench with Jerome and hadn't spoken since we launched.

Tater turned left and steered us across a pool of chemicals, or oil, or something else unnatural, floating like a poisonous lily pad. When we cleared it, I looked down to see us passing directly over a submerged teeter-totter.

"Look." Jerome pointed to the charred remains of a home. "Burned not a month before Katrina. I knew those people. They were goin' to rebuild."

I took more photos.

We sailed on.

A snake slithered by gracefully, cutting a perfect wake through the shiny brown water next to our boat.

A rescue team in a much larger boat was smashing in the door of a three-story home with the words, HELP! 3 STILL ALIVE! painted on the front door. I doubted it. We were out of sight before I would ever know.

"Over there. That's Fats Domino's place." Jerome pointed.

"That's right, I remember seeing him on TV being rescued by a helicopter."

"One of New Awlins finest," Jez said.

Jerome said an amen and fished a life preserver out of the water with an oar.

From behind me, Bela gasped and cried out.

"What?"

To our right, we saw a white man floating faceup in sweatpants and a yellow T-shirt. He was tied to a telephone pole by two ropes around his ankles. The corpse was so bloated that its shirt stretched tight across the chest and belly as if five sizes too small, ready to burst at the seams.

I felt my chest tighten and I nervously cracked my knuckles.

"Closer, Tater. Please."

He maneuvered the boat in a wide circle and pulled up close to the body, carefully avoiding the ropes that kept it from drifting onto someone's porch.

I think my cell phone rang inside my front pocket.

Tater stepped over me and past Bela and Jez to the transom. He killed the motor.

Jerome stood.

"Careful," Jez said.

Not him, I thought when we were close enough to see.

Jerome looked down at the dead man's face.

"You know him?"

"No," Jerome answered.

"Nine or ten days, I bet you," Jez said. "That's how long that poor man has been there."

I watched Joe lean over and throw up over the side of the boat.

Jerome closely examined the ruins of nearby houses. "No way of knowing how far he walked—or drifted—before being tied up here."

I put my camera to my eye and pushed the shutter halfway down. The image was more clear and colorful and moving than anything I'd seen through my lens in a long time.

I put the camera back in my lap.

Bela was crying. I turned around again. She had her head down as Jez rubbed her back.

"It's OK, he's in a better place, sweet girl. Don't cry. It's OK."

"Familiar to anyone else?"

No, no, and no.

"Start it up," Jerome said.

As we chugged away, Jerome pointed to the sky and whispered a prayer whose words I could not hear.

Another flat-bottom boat passed by us. Two men in Coast Guard jackets stood inside. Four body bags lay across the boat's benches.

No waves, no hellos, no salutes, just a solemn nod. An acknowledgement.

You're doing work few men or women could, I thought.

A helicopter flew overhead. Then another. Then a third. The last flew low enough to send ripples through the water. I wondered if they'd reach the corpse behind us.

"There," Jerome said. He pointed with the oar to a two-story house three houses down on our right and sitting on a corner lot.

Again I turned. Bela was rubbing her forehead, adjusting her cap. "That's it," she said.

"My dad's?"

"Mm-hmm."

This time Hamp came back and turned off the motor just as we cleared what I judged to be a four-foot chain-link fence. We crossed over the edge of what should have been a front lawn.

The water covered the raised porch and lapped about two feet up against the front door. The water had receded in this area more than most, but was still easily eight feet deep. Most of the home's shingles were gone. A gutter hung vertically in a tree, its bottom some fifteen feet off the ground.

Tater guided the boat up to the porch railing and tied it securely.

"I found fishing waders for three."

"Bela, Jez, and Cherie should have them." I spoke up quickly. They didn't argue.

I steadied Bela so she could put on the military-green waders that came to her hips. "You don't have to come in," I said.

"I know. But I am."

I took Bela's hand and helped her out of the boat.

Then I helped Jez don her pair of waders.

Cherie pulled hers on so quickly and with such ease everyone but her husband Joe stopped to gawk.

"Fly-fishing," she said.

We each put on our industrial-strength gloves.

Tater had opened a window in the front that led into the living room. The men climbed through first. The water was cold and murky, but the smell I'd expected to knock me over was actually tolerable.

We helped the women through the window.

I surveyed the living room. Nails in plaster where pictures had hung. Overturned furniture. Lime-green plastic plates. An upside-down microwave. A container of Tupperware filled with red beans was still sealed tight.

"A lot of stuff was taken upstairs, I figure." Jerome's husky voice seemed even more authoritative inside the house. "Your dad lived in a room upstairs."

"Did he have roommates?" I asked as Jerome led us up the stairs.

"He did. The guy who owned the place, Jardine, was a Corvette mechanic, of all things. His specialty, I guess. And another guy, but he hadn't been here very long."

There were more empty nails on the walls near the bottom of the stairs, but three photos closer to the top had survived.

One was of Dad, beaming, clear-eyed, and standing behind a group of children holding instruments and kneeling in a line across the foot of a dimly lit stage. Dad had less hair than I'd remembered.

The second, hanging almost sideways on the nail, showed me, Dad, and Billy Crystal in a parking lot. I was clutching an auto-graphed pennant.

The third, and closest to the top of the stairs, was of Dad and a radiant Jez showing off a very modest diamond ring. They were sitting on a step at the same fountain where I'd met the British couple. In the professionally printed photo they'd added the text:

CHARLIE AND JEZ: JUST ENGAGED

"I love that one," Jez said, walking by it and putting her left hand lightly on the glass. She admired her ring again. "I've got a copy of that one, too."

I had just barely arrived at the top of the stairs when Jerome called our attention.

"Oh, my," Jerome said. He stood in an open doorway at the end of the hallway, staring into a room with a stunned look on his face.

He's dead.

I don't know quite why, but I looked at my watch and slowly walked down the hallway. I looked at Jez in front; she seemed unfazed. Behind me Bela was walking with her gloved hands thrust deep in her pockets.

Tater and Hamp were farther down the hallway.

Joe and Cherie had waited downstairs.

It was not as I had pictured the moment, but not so far removed from my imagination that it felt like a dream.

I continued walking. Other doors were shut. The attic access door was open, but the ladder had been folded back onto itself.

Rest in peace, Dad.

I arrived at the open door and Jerome stepped to the side, allowing me access.

I stepped inside. The room was empty.

I saw only a bed without sheets and a dresser with the drawers hanging out and empty.

"This was your dad's room," Jerome said.

It looked like someone had become bored with the Big Easy and moved out on a weekend whim.

I looked back to the doorway. Jez stood with her hands on her hips and the most puzzled look on her face.

"What happened, Jerome?" I asked. "You sure this was my dad's room?"

"Of course," Jerome insisted. "Helped him get this dresser up here."

"You said you looked in his room."

"We did, son. Castle checked it himself. It looked like a regular room. His belongin's were here. Everythin'."

From the hallway we heard the attic ladder being lowered. I barely had time to walk down the hallway, considering why my dad's room was bare, before Tater and Hamp were disappearing into the dark hole in the ceiling.

"Jerome!" Tater yelled. "Go get a flashlight from the boat. In the box under the seat up front."

"I've got one," Bela said, tossing it up to Hamp.

His big hands cradled and caught it perfectly. "Luke," he said.

"Yeah?"

"Climb up."

Halfway up the stairs, I was high enough to see what Tater illuminated in a single column of light.

Groups of plastic bags, sealed tightly with duct tape. Two suitcases, a Rubbermaid tub I knew held letters from my mother, a guitar case, and several small, unlabeled cardboard boxes.

I was looking at every single thing my father owned.

Wrapped in Dad's emergency trash bags and duct tape.

Dry.

CHAPTER
25

I
t took half an hour to load everything on the flat-bottom boat. Hamp, Jerome, Joe, and Cherie all insisted on staying back, willing to wait for a second run, so we could take Dad's belongings in one trip. Jerome gave Jez the keys to the van and gave us a shove off the porch.

I sat between Jez and Bela on the last bench. Bela held my hand and Jez once again looped one of her arms through mine.

Tater got us back to the staging area in just ten minutes.

We loaded the bags, boxes, and guitar into the van, and Tater returned to pick up the others. Jez suggested I remove my shoes and socks, throw my socks away, and wash my feet in bottled water.

Jez drove Bela and me back down to Rampart, past the police command posts and Red Cross tents, past the mountains of trash, and right through the red lights. It crossed my mind I hadn't seen anyone stop for a red light or stop sign since I'd arrived.

Jez maneuvered the van with ease down the narrow alley, and

we quickly unloaded everything through the kitchen onto several tables in the bar.

"Back soon. I'll get the others." Jez hugged me again. I didn't think she'd ever left or entered a room without putting her arms around me.

Bela found a box cutter and a steak knife and we each began surgically cutting away at the duct tape and plastic bags.

"I don't think any of us expected this," Bela said.

"Finding his things?"

"Yeah."

"Isn't that the truth," I said. "I'm beginning to wonder if he's not still alive after all. Twenty thousand-plus people went to Houston. Others to New Mexico, Arizona, Georgia, the Carolinas— they're everywhere." I felt excited, even hopeful.

Bela continued cutting away layers of tape on a shoebox.

"Don't you think?" I asked.

"I don't know what I think anymore."

"I thought you were the confident one. The optimist."

"I am." She looked up at me, but only long enough for our eyes to meet, then she concentrated on her box again. "But I'm also a realist."

"How do you explain this? How do you explain Jerome and the others checking Dad's place and seeing his stuff one day, then nothing the next. Maybe he came back home as the water was rising, bagged up his things, saving his stuff like he always thought he would, and ended up getting taken on some boat or bus or plane out of the city."

Bela had her back to me. But her shoulders said she was crying.

"Bela?" I turned her around. "What's wrong?"

She was holding a photo of my father and Jezebel in Jackson Square surrounded by a giddy-looking group of kids toting trumpets, trombones, and tubas. Dad had an arm around his fiancée and a smile on his face that dominated the photo.

I put my arms around Bela and whispered, "Shhh. It's all right."

After a minute or two, Bela pulled away and wiped her eyes. She missed a tear that stopped on the edge of her perfect jawline.

I wiped it away for her.

We returned to the task of discovering what Dad had left behind.

More pictures, a hundred or more, in a Ziploc bag in a shoebox that had been taped shut and then wrapped in plastic that had *also* been taped shut.

CDs, mostly jazz.

A journal I'd never known he kept during Mom's last year.

Two watches.

Newspaper and magazine clippings of wire-service photos. *Mine.*

A Troy Aikman autographed mini-football.

Mom's keychain collection with a tiny guitar from Nashville, a hand-carved wooden bear that said SAN FRAN, and others from Tallahassee, Tampa, Atlanta, San Antonio, Chicago, Phoenix.

A burgundy, leather-bound scrapbook. I untied the white ribbon keeping it closed.

"Jez made that for your dad."

"Jez?"

"Uh-huh. We sat right over there." She pointed to the farthest corner table under a picture of Archie Manning.

I opened the book to an 8x10 of Dad and Jez on a swamp boat. I flipped the page to concert tickets. "Snoop Dogg?"

Bela snickered. "Yeah, Jezebel has eclectic taste."

I flipped a page. Two soft-drink labels from plastic twelve-ounce bottles were placed next to a picture of my father and Jez standing in front of the JW Marriott on Canal during Mardi Gras. They were both holding Pepsi bottles.

I turned another page. NBA tickets and an extremely long shoelace under a plastic page protector. I looked at Bela questioningly.

"Shaq. Your dad took me to a Hornets game on my birthday."

"That's quite a gift," I said.

I turned more pages. A restaurant menu, a chord chart, an ace of spades, a handwritten poem on a Verses napkin. A picture of Dad and Castle standing and smiling outside a nondescript building with a sign that was too small to read. Every piece of Dad's treasure was safely guarded behind the thick page protectors.

A feather. An empty bag of Planters peanuts. A white sheet of paper with the Alcoholics Anonymous' well-known Twelve Steps written out by hand.

"Take it out," Bela said.

I did, and she took it from me and turned it over.

"That's his list. Step Eight," she said.

I read aloud. "'Number Eight: Made a list of all persons we had harmed, and became willing to make amends to them all.'" Beneath those words were names scribbled in Dad's handwriting. "Kaiser, Erin, Lee, Jamie, the Halladays, Spencer, Roberta, Mrs. Robitaille, the Bellamys, Patrick, John R., Tiff, Lonnie, Summer, the Mangums, Laurie S., the Fleeks, Mary Ann . . ." I didn't read the last name aloud.

Luke.

"I don't recognize most of these," I said.

"Me either, though I've heard about Lee. He was one of your dad's A.A. sponsors in Texas."

"Didn't go so well?" I asked.

"Ask Jez," she said. "And John"—she put her finger on his name for emphasis—"John was a sponsor too, but only for a couple of meetings. I met him when Charlie first hit New Awlins. Nice guy."

I scanned the list again. "We had a neighbor in Texas—the

Bellamys, this must be them. I wonder what Dad needed to make right."

"Not for us to know. But I'll tell you why this list is in a scrapbook and not in his pocket." She smiled wisdom. "Because he had these names memorized, and he'd tried to find time for every one of them to make things better."

"Did they accept?"

"Jez would know better than me, but I don't think everyone returned his calls." She hesitated. "I know he's sure been trying."

I slid the paper back into the scrapbook and flipped the page.

I saw a collage of Dad and Jez in every imaginable New Orleans setting with the location written in Jez's careful handwriting below each picture. It covered two pages.

The zoo. Armstrong Park. Louisiana Children's Museum. Houmas House Plantation and Gardens. The French Market. A WWII museum. Wearing masks aboard the Creole Queen. Inside the Pharmacy Museum.

"The Pharmacy Museum?" I asked.

"Yep, it's right down the street."

"I can't believe some of the things Jezebel got my dad to do."

"You have no idea," she said. "True love, I guess." She stood. "You thirsty? I'm hiding some Sierra Mist in the back."

"Is it warm?"

"Very."

"Perfect."

She walked into the kitchen and returned a moment later with two cans and two glasses.

"Hey, Luke, tell me about your dad's premonitions."

"Haven't we had this conversation?"

"No, we haven't."

That's right, I remembered. *That was Jordan.*

"Is this one of those routines where I tell you a story you already know?"

She smiled. I was beginning to like it when she smiled in my direction.

"Fair. How about I tell one *you* don't know."

I poured my soda and took a drink. It made me realize how hungry I actually was. I opened the second can and poured it in Bela's glass.

"Your dad had a premonition—"

"Dream."

"Whatever. They're inseparable, aren't they?"

I let it go. After all, I *was* sitting at a table covered with boxes wrapped in plastic bags and duct tape.

"Keep going." I took another drink. The sugar tasted terrific on my tongue.

"Your dad had one. About you."

"I think he had a lot about me, Bel."

I liked that.

She rolled her eyes.

I think she did, too.

"Maybe he did. But this was recent. He told the whole club about it. Heck, I bet he told his roommates, his guys at Jackson Square. Everyone. I wouldn't be surprised if he'd called Jim Haslett."

"The Saints' head coach? Please." I snickered. "I get it. He told people."

"He said he'd had the strongest premonition, or dream, or inspiration—you pick—of his life."

I sat a little straighter in my chair.

"He said that one day he'd show you the city he'd come to love."

"That could be any—"

"No. It was *this* one. He said one day you'd come. He'd take you around town just like Jez has taken you around. Take the pictures and build a page for your scrapbook just like this one." She placed her hand on the open page. "He said you'd see him differently, see what he'd done here, see who he'd become . . ." Bela's eyes welled up with tears. This time she didn't wipe them away.

I reached across the table and took her hand in mine.

"Luke, your dad, Charlie—he was not the man you remember."

"Does that mean he was sober? Designing buildings again? Free from guilt about my mother?" The answers suddenly mattered.

Bela's breathing was labored.

"I'm getting it, Bel, that's why I think he's out there. I think maybe he's out there *waiting* to work it out. Somehow, somewhere. Maybe there's a second chance for us after all. I can't help but think what an idiot I've been . . ."

Bela stood and this time engaged me in a long, warm hug that lasted forever and yet, somehow, not nearly long enough. If either of us smelled of Katrina, we wouldn't have known it.

"Luke, I want you to know how much it helps me to think that even though we lost your dad, we found you." She paused. "I found you."

"Not so fast, Bela. This isn't over yet. *I still believe.*"

She took both my hands and squeezed "You're a good man. . . . I'll be back later."

"Soon?"

She nodded and wiped her nose on the back of her hand with as much grace as possible.

"You're OK by yourself?"

She nodded again and left.

I opened the rest of the boxes and bags, at least enough to tell what was inside. Clothes, another scrapbook I set aside to open later, more photos, A.A. pins marking numbers of days sober. An 8½x11 pencil rendering of our home in Dallas. The home he dreamt he'd build for Mom.

I found a baseball cap in another Ziploc bag. Yankees.

The one thing I most wanted to see, the thing I'd considered *praying* to find in one of the larger boxes, was missing.

"Dad's sax," I said aloud.

I pushed the worry aside, picked up the baseball cap, and hiked the spiral staircase to my bedroom in the hallway. I powered up my laptop to download the day's pictures. My battery was down to fifty percent and I'd forgotten to bring a spare. I hoped I'd either see power again or maybe a turn at the generator on the patio behind the club.

At such high resolution, the photos imported slowly. I set the computer down on the couch and went back downstairs to find something dry and edible. I helped myself to some Pop-Tarts and a single-serving package of Fig Newtons. I hated Fig Newtons.

I returned upstairs and gave myself a two-minute sponge bath in the bathroom. Then I put on the cleanest clothes I had left. Comfortable slacks and a long-sleeved shirt I had worn on my trip to Peru. It was a surprisingly comfortable outfit for a hot, humid climate like Louisiana. I used the restroom and said a humble prayer of thanksgiving that there was still toilet paper. Then I covered my wet-mop hair with Dad's baseball cap and shut the bathroom door behind me.

It was time to settle in to view the pictures from our Lower Ninth expedition. A few weren't usable, or at least not of professional reprint quality, but a dozen or so jumped off the screen and begged to be sent to Kirky, my agent back in Manhattan.

I scrolled backward to the pictures I'd shown Bela earlier. A few were good enough, I expected, to end up on the wire or in a magazine. I'd get the whole bunch to Kirky as soon as I found my father.

Alive? I thought.

Some were too tragic to share. One or two were so distasteful I was ashamed for having taking them at all and deleted them from both my laptop and my camera.

I pulled up the funeral picture I'd brushed past when Bela had been sitting next to me. Viewing it full-size overwhelmed my screen. I reduced it to fifty percent, still large enough to see more detail than I had on the camera itself or in the iPhoto preview window.

There were more people on the street that day than I'd noticed at the time. I blew the photo up to sixty percent and dragged the image up to see the men at the front of the march.

The one who played the trombone looked like my new friend, Tater.

Odd.

I dragged the picture down slightly. One of the two men on trumpet looked like Hamp. I felt like a fool for not discovering those two had been at a funeral that day, just an hour or two before I'd first arrived.

I blew the photo up to seventy percent. One man stood taller than the rest.

Castle?

I tried eighty-five percent. Jerome and two other men I didn't know were also playing instruments. A white man and a black man carried the casket.

One hundred percent. A woman in a white T-shirt walked near the back of the march. *Bela.*

She stood by another woman. *Jezebel.* She was sobbing and carrying a large photo.

Enlarged at two hundred percent, even through the grainy dots of distance and light and utter disbelief, I recognized instantly the photo she held:

CHARLIE AND JEZ: JUST ENGAGED

PART 3

CHAPTER
26

My father is dead.

I looked at the photo again, enlarging it even more and dragging the photo around the screen until I saw a close-up of every familiar face.

Jerome. The man who brought me here.

Jezebel. My father's fiancée.

Castle. Was his sister really dying in D.C.?

My father is dead.

Tater and Hamp. One was more talkative than the other. Was the other not part of the lie?

Joe and Cherie. Reluctant?

Bela.

My heart broke.

Footsteps on the first floor. Quiet conversation. I'd just spent three days in the city looking for a man they already knew was dead. They had deceived me, all of them. Was Frank Rostron part of it, too?

With haste I packed my duffel and zipped up my camera and laptop bags. I walked into the bathroom and splashed water on my face. I rubbed my hand through my week-old beard. I'd forgotten how much I looked like my father when I didn't shave.

I've spent three days as a fool.

I debated punishing or trapping them. I picked up my bags and stood at the top of the stairs. I could tell them my girlfriend called. "Great news," I might say. "They found my father alive in San Antonio! I'm leaving right this second to go find him. Who wants to come!"

Then I'd rush out the door straight for New York City.

The idea floated away as quickly as I'd thought it.

My father was dead.

I was crying.

If I ever married, he wouldn't be there. If I had children, he wouldn't be sitting there anxiously in the waiting room, waiting for me to present him with his grandchild and tell him the baby's name. He'd never promise to spoil the baby he'd never meet.

Was Mom waiting for him?

I cried harder.

What if he had changed and wanted me back in his life? What if we were willing to love each other again? Now I'd never know.

If he was dead, I could never look into his clear eyes and ask him to love me, if he could.

I placed my head against the wall and muffled my cries in the crook of my arm. I missed a man I'd all but given up on. I'd prepared for this. Numbed myself. Conjured up memories of a drunken father ruining my graduation, wrecking my car, begging for my money.

I missed my father.

I went back to the bathroom and washed my face again. *Show them the photo.* I pulled out my laptop once again. It was still on. I opened it and walked down the stairs. My hands were shaking.

"Hey, sweetheart." Jez was pulling Red Cross meals from a box and handing them out. "You hungry?"

She didn't notice or care that I hadn't answered because she asked Bela the same question just a few seconds later.

The increasingly attentive Bela must have noticed I'd been crying. She walked up to me. The laptop was still open in my arms, the image of Jez and her fountain photo enlarged to nearly life-size.

"You all right, Luke?"

"Absolutely."

I set the laptop down on the end of the bar, pointed the photo at Jez, and walked back up the stairs for my bags.

"Where you goin'?" Jerome's voice boomed. "You must be dyin' of hunger."

I collected my things, made a quick pass through the couch cushions, hallway, and bathroom for anything I might have left or dropped. Then I stopped at the top of the stairs for a few minutes and listened.

It didn't take long for the front door to open. I saw Tater, Hamp, Joe, and Cherie slinking out. It looked like Cherie had both hands over her mouth. Joe had his arm around her.

I inhaled and took the steps deliberately, like each one mattered. I thought of Jordan.

I wish she was here.

The second my foot hit the bottom step Jezebel swarmed me and pulled me in tight. I didn't set down my bags. I just stood there.

Next to the laptop, Jerome held a shaking, sobbing Bela. Jerome comforted her, or tried, but she couldn't have heard him over her own cries.

Jezebel was still holding me. "I'm so sorry, Luke."

I'd already decided to leave without saying anything more than the photo had already revealed. I'd be strong. I'd be like my dad would have been. I waited to move until Jezebel finally dropped her arms. She backed off and looked at me. Her cheeks were shiny, soaked, and a little dirty.

"I'm sorry," she said again. "We'll explain."

Bela couldn't have explained anything. She was inconsolable.

I pulled my laptop from the bar, shut it down, and put it in my bag. I took the three steps to the front door.

"Luke," Jerome bellowed like never before. "Don't walk out that door without knowing. Don't walk out."

"*Stop,*" Jezebel plead. "Just a minute. Listen, *please. Please* turn around."

I did, but only because I knew my dad wouldn't ever walk away from someone talking to him. Not even a screaming, berating, belittling wife.

But I remained silent.

"This was your dad's wish," Jezebel said.

For you to lie?

I looked at Bela. She'd calmed a bit and was sitting on the same barstool I'd been occupying for three days.

"It was for you to see his city, to discover him."

How could you possibly know that?

"Luke, I bet you didn't know your father completed A.A.," Jerome said from behind the bar. He opened a bottle of water for Bela.

"He knew," Bela whispered.

Jez took the pulpit again. "That's right, Luke. It took trying and failing every place he'd ever been. But right here, here in the Crescent City, Charlie did it."

"Castle sponsored him," Jerome said. "He did wonders. Led him through everythin'. Castle's been sober four years himself."

I looked at Bela. She tried to smile, but could only nod agreement and look down.

How did he die? I wanted to ask, but decided it would wait.

Jez took my bags off my shoulders and set them on the floor.

I don't know why I didn't resist.

"Do you have any clue—any clue at all—how badly your father wanted a new life? He left every bit he could of that old self in Texas. He came here and ate up music instead. He came here to a clean slate. He struggled like nobody's business, but that man did it. We did it *together.*"

I looked away from her and toward the photos on the wall.

"Luke, you're not understanding us, sweetheart. Or not listening. Or both. Your father loved you. That's why he stopped calling. You remember that? You remember asking him not to?"

Don't.

"He heard you loud and clear and it stung, Luke. Charlie came to New Awlins lonely and afraid and broke. But that saxophone of his brought him to Jackson Square." She become emotional again. The tears were back and so was the heartbreaking shine on her face. "And Jackson Square led him to Jerome and to Verses and to me. And as sure as our city is crying, as sure as you see me standing here, I knew I loved your dad from the second I saw him. And he felt exactly the same. True love."

On that we agree.

"Are you going to speak, young man?" Jerome's voice filled the bar.

I looked at him with more than a little fear in my chest.

"Just know," Jez rolled on, "this was the hardest thing I've ever done. It's about killed sweet Bela. But it was your father's *last wish*—his final dream—that you would forgive him and discover his second verse."

I picked up my bags and walked to the door. Jezebel hugged me from behind one final time. As I stepped across the threshold, I looked over my shoulder to see Bela standing by the bar.

"Luke," she managed to whisper. "You were my O.G.T. in all this. My One Good Thing."

I wanted desperately to tell her the same thing.

Instead I turned and walked out the door.

When I was about a block away, I pulled out my phone and sent Jordan a text message:

DAD GONE. COMING HOME.

I looked at my watch: 6:30 PM. I wondered where Jordan might be for the first time since I'd left.

Then I sent a second message:

CALL ME

By 6:31 my phone was vibrating.

"I'm so sorry, Luke." Total devotion in her voice.

"Hey, Jordy."

"So he's gone?"

"Yeah."

"How?"

"Don't know exactly. Only that he's dead and there's been a funeral."

"That fast? Were you there?"

"Sort of."

"Come home and tell me about it."

"I will, but I need something in the meantime."

"Of course. Anything."

I pulled Jerome's cell phone number from my address book and gave it to Jordan. I gave her a thinned-down version of what I'd experienced the first three days as well as the last sixty minutes.

"I'm not sure I understand."

"You will."

I asked her to call Jerome's number as many times as it took for him to answer, and then to politely ask for Jezebel.

"Remember what you told me the other day?" I asked quietly.

"About?"

"About doing something for me? About believing in me?"

"Of course."

"I need you."

"Of course, Luke."

"When Jezebel is on the phone, tell her who you are. Tell her you're calling for details about my father's death. Where his remains are. Any circumstances at all. Tell her I need to know so I can put my father to rest. Names, numbers, whatever she can tell you."

"Shouldn't you have done this?"

"It's complicated." *Pride is a complicated animal.*

"OK, so get what I can get from this woman."

"She's the one I told you about. She was engaged to Dad."

"Oh." Jordan was quiet for a moment. "When will you be home?"

"Three days. Hattiesburg tonight, Blacksburg, Virginia, tomorrow, and then New York."

"Same route?"

"It is."

"All right."

"You'll call her?"

"I will. Drive safe."

"Don't worry if I don't call, all right?"

"All right."

I thanked her and hung up.

I was surprised at how easily I remembered the route back to my car. On the way, I stopped by the Red Cross tent on Canal Street. When no one was available to help, I simply walked over to a pallet full of empty body bags, grabbed two, swiped a half-empty can of spray paint from a folding table, and continued on my way.

When I got to the bridge, I was thankful the two sleeping men's bodies were fragile and dry.

Nothing dramatic. Just two men—brothers, friends, maybe strangers—who fell asleep under a bridge and never woke up. I loaded them each in a bag and dragged them to the center of the road.

I spray-painted a giant circle around the bodies with arrows pointing to them from all directions. Then I said a prayer. Not a Jerome prayer, just a Millward prayer. "God help them."

My rental car was untouched. *A small miracle,* I thought, *in a city that ran out of miracles for me.*

I drove out of town like I knew exactly where I was going.

CHAPTER
27

The drive home was divinely uneventful.

I slept in my car at the Hattiesburg Holiday Inn Express. I stayed at a very familiar Best Western in Virginia and took a twenty-five-minute shower.

By sundown on the second full day I was fighting traffic in the city.

I'd decided not to talk to Jordan on the way home. We sent a handful of text messages. She sent that she'd had success with the "project" and would fill me in when I got home.

For the first time since I was sixteen I actually chose to drive in the slow lane. I spent miles imagining a heroic death for my father. I suppose I hoped he'd had one of his premonitions about his death before Katrina hit.

What if he had? What if he wasn't heroic? When have I been this conflicted?

I was angry. Dad had agreed to have me search in the dark.

Even suggested it. Would a call or letter from Jez have been any different? Why had Bela lied to me? Had her loyalty to my father been so strong?

Some of the questions lodged in my mind. Others ran through my mind, past my mouth, and into the air.

I wished someone were there to hear them.

My mind, still numb from the images of my stay in New Awlins, conjured up and sorted through a hundred and fifty miles of circumstances for my father's death.

Drowned in a neighbor's attic, trying to pull them to safety.

Drowned in Jezebel's attic, trying to pull *her* to safety.

Stabbed at the Convention Center, killed while protecting a child.

Electrocuted.

Burned to death, saving a family pet from a burning home in the Garden District.

Crushed by a pickup truck that rushed with the storm surge over the canal breech. Dad swimming furiously to push a woman and her baby in an inner tube from the truck's path.

Drowned by a woman he was trying to save. Her frantic, panicked motions drowning them both.

Heat exhaustion. Collapsed from an arduous trip to the Convention Center. He delivered a woman in a wheelchair in time to find oxygen. Because of Dad's speed she was one of the lucky ones who received medical attention in time. Dad stayed with the widow until she boarded a bus for Houston. Alive and thankful.

Some scenarios made me feel better than others. But all were more appealing than imagining my father had been found behind Circus Circus in Las Vegas with a gunshot wound and a gambling debt.

I turned on the radio and listened to classic rock until I rolled through the Lincoln Tunnel.

It was after seven when I returned the rental car in Greenwich Village and got in a cab. I was exhausted, dirty, and ready to bury my father in every appropriate way.

I hoped Jordan would be waiting for me.

"Knock, knock." I opened the front door to my clean, dry apartment. It looked precisely as it had when I had left.

Except that there was a woman sitting next to Jordan on my futon.

Jezebel.

CHAPTER
28

Jezebel hugged me.

What else could I expect? She held on to me and sniffled through a "Hello, I'm relieved you made it. So relieved" before stepping back.

"Jordan?"

"Welcome home." She held me in a long, warm embrace. "I think you know Jezebel," she said when the hug ended too soon.

"Uh." I kept looking at Jezebel and wondering if I'd eaten bad Mexican fast food at the place in Blacksburg. "What's going on?"

"Sit down."

"OK," I said dumbly, and I did.

I finally realized that the smell coming from my kitchen was jambalaya. Once I noticed it, I couldn't ignore it. If it tasted even a fraction as well as it smelled, I knew I was going to sleep very well on a very full stomach.

Jezebel sat on the other end of the futon.

Jordan sat between us.

The three of us were sitting on a futon made for two.

Jordan sat up straight. "Luke, I spoke to Jezebel."

"Uh-huh."

"She refused to tell me anything, *anything,* over the phone."

Color me surprised. "So you invited her for dinner?"

Jezebel tried not to laugh but a snort most definitely escaped.

"Not quite. She invited herself."

I couldn't avoid noticing Jezebel had taken a shower. Her hair still looked slightly damp.

"How did you get here?" I asked her.

"Airplane. They reopened the airport, just enough flights a day to get a few people in and out."

"How did you get to my place?"

"Luke," Jordan cut Jezebel off, "I picked her up at the airport."

I stood up, not out of anger, but because the sideways conservation on the futon was as awkward as the discussion. "And did I pay for her plane ticket?"

Now Jezebel stood. "What? You think because I'm black and from New Awlins I can't buy my own plane ticket?" She had the same look in her eyes I'd seen when she nearly gave a beating to Officer Baldy at Jackson Square.

"Relax. I didn't know if you had your credit cards—"

"Oh, no, Citibank don't give 'dem credit cards to no *Negro* women—"

"Stop it you two!" Jordan stood up as well, forcing us into a tighter circle than any of us liked. In unison we all took a step back.

"Jez—" Jordan started.

"'Jez'? You're calling her Jez already?" I interrupted. Jordan hated to be interrupted.

"Luke Francis Millward. Stop. This is inappropriate. Just stop. All of it. Both of you."

She was right. Suddenly I felt like I was twelve again. And I didn't entirely mind it. Perhaps it was only fair for Jezebel to get what I'd spared her in New Orleans.

"Jezebel." Jordan was about to negotiate. She looked at me for a nod at using her full first name. I gave it.

"Luke didn't mean anything you just implied. You know that. He meant that he wasn't sure you'd have access to your funds, to your credit cards, debit cards." Then she turned to me.

"Luke, are you paying any attention? First, you didn't buy her ticket. I did. We're not married and you didn't leave me an emergency VISA like I'm some sixteen-year-old kid. I bought it. She can pay me back when she gets home. I'm sure she will."

"Naturally," Jez said. Nice and snide.

"Secondly, Luke, have you looked past the surprise of seeing this beautiful woman on your couch to even wonder why she came?"

I had, but I wasn't sure I was ready to hear it.

"Jez, could you check on that delicious-smelling dinner you've started? I need a moment with Luke."

Jez walked past me into the kitchen, all of fifteen feet away. Jordan pulled me into my bathroom and shut the door.

"Luke. Please listen to her. For me?"

"She lied, Jordan. They *all* lied."

"I get that. Be mad at her later, but she's traveled all the way up here for more than a shower."

She hugged me again.

"After dinner."

"Fair." She kissed me on the cheek. "You OK?"

"I'm starving."

We ate dinner and made small talk. Very small.

Jordan talked about her week, her clients, her boss, and makeup.

Jez talked about her flight up and the last time she'd been to New York. It had been just a few months ago for a show. I wondered if my dad had come, too.

I talked about the drive there and back. Jez hadn't heard any of it and looked sincerely interested. I wanted to ask about Bela, but didn't.

After dinner Jordan offered—*insisted*—on cleaning up. "That was the most fantastic meal I've had in a year. I mean it."

"Thank you, sweetheart. It's just simple Cajun cooking."

Jordan was still mumbling about it when she took the last of the dishes and placed them by the sink. She began washing them by hand, despite my owning a very nice dishwasher.

"Why don't you two go for a walk; it's gorgeous outside."

I looked at Jez. She shrugged.

I shrugged back.

Jez snorted again. "You're too much. Let's go." She walked out the door without looking back.

She was still standing in front of the notoriously slow elevator when I caught up with her.

"Two elevators," I said. "One is slow, one is broken all the time."

Jez reached down and pushed the button again. "I hear this works," she said.

"I've heard that, too." I counted to five and pressed the button again. "Jez, I'm sorry about that. Back there. The credit card thing."

"It's OK. We're blowing off steam."

I had to wonder what steam *she* was storing. I was the one who'd been shammed. "Right," I wisely said instead.

The elevator arrived and we rode down to the first floor. The doorman held the front door for us.

"That would take some getting used to," she said.

"I never quite have," I fibbed. Actually I'd been in the city long enough to take it for granted.

We began walking east for no apparent reason, but before we left the block I stopped her. "Mind if we just sit?" I motioned to a nearby bench.

"Are you kidding me? I'm so exhausted. I couldn't believe that girl of yours suggested a walk. I've been on my feet for almost two weeks." It wasn't easy to collapse onto a metal bench, but Jezebel tried.

"Much better." I sat next to her.

We sat quietly for a few moments.

"You flew in today?"

"This morning. Jordan's wonderful, Luke."

"Thanks."

More silence.

"I have a story to tell you."

"I know."

"It's why I came."

"I know."

"Your dad was a wonderful man, Luke. And I loved him with all my heart."

"I see it." I looked her in the eyes. "I see it."

"If Charlie Millward had asked me to travel to the ends of the earth just to turn around and come home, I'd have done it. So long as he was by my side." She took a breath and rubbed her face.

"I am *not* going to cry anymore." She took another breath and continued.

"The day the storm hit, that night really, we all stayed in the club. We thought there was a decent chance the Quarter would stay dry. We were right. But before the storm had even passed, your dad said he needed to leave. Couldn't have been 5:00 AM yet. Was still raining pretty good. But he said he needed to get home to the Lower Ninth. There was no stopping him. Trust me, we all tried."

She clucked at a pigeon walking within a few feet of her and carrying a piece of a soft-baked pretzel.

"He took a cell phone and promised to call, said he'd be OK, said the worst was past and we'd dodged the bullet. Shoot, that's what the TV was saying right up until the levees tumbled and flooded us."

"How did Dad get there?"

"He walked."

"All the way home?"

"It's only three miles or so and he had a flashlight in both pockets. He called when he hit the neighborhood and said he needed to help a neighbor. Must have helped another and another because Jerome got worried when the rain started to lighten up but Charlie hadn't come back yet."

"And Dad's place was like he left it."

"That's right," she nodded. "He hadn't been there yet."

"So sometime between Jerome checking his place and the levees breaking he got in there . . . He knew the levees would break."

"Mm-hmm. He knew," she agreed. "We never spoke to him again. A day or so later when we really started to worry, you know, we hoped he'd somehow ended up in Texas or Georgia or somewhere. I would have been angry, and Lord knows I would have told him so, but he'd have been alive, right? Anyway, when he hadn't called or come back to the Quarter, Jerome called you."

"And you didn't know *anything* then?"

"Nothing."

"Really?"

"Nothing, Luke. We were looking and we were praying—*Lord* did we pray."

"So when did you find him?"

"Two days before you arrived. But Luke, we didn't think you were coming."

"Why? I said I was."

"Come on, Luke, this is me. Be real with me. You dragged your feet and you know it."

Maybe a little.

"You weren't in a rush were you? You were not in any big hurry to come recover your alcoholic father."

"OK. I get it."

"Luke, I'm telling you the truth, sweetheart. We did not think you were coming. We were stunned. We'd just had Charlie's funeral and then you come waltzing in."

"Why so soon, Jez? No one was holding funerals yet."

"Because we didn't think you were coming, and Castle, the man who sponsored your dad and helped free him from the bottle, was leaving to be with his sister. He wanted to be a part of it so much, Luke. So we put our ragtag funeral march together. I don't much care if anyone thinks we should have waited, no offense. It was a simple celebration."

"So where did you bury him?"

"We didn't. We couldn't. The casket was empty. They do that from time to time down there. FEMA had put him in a freezer and said there was nothing we could do with him right now. Wasn't a funeral home open for probably five hundred miles." She slid over and put an arm around me. "I'm sorry to tell you like this, to talk like he was just another victim of this mess."

"So when can I retrieve him?"

"Oh. Well, sweetheart, if you bury him outside the area you can recover Charles right now."

"But you want him buried in New Orleans."

"No."

"Why not?"

"I want him buried next to his wife, Luke. That's who the Lord ordained as his spouse, for better or worse. I'll live knowing my world was changed by the six months I spent with him."

I appreciated the gesture more than I could explain, but my mind was already on *the* question I needed answered most.

"How did he die?"

Jez took my hand. "You know we couldn't reach him; cell service got bad in a hurry. Spotty. Sometimes you got through, usually you didn't. Texts were better, but even that was so hit-and-miss. Finally after a couple days of not hearing anything, an officer came by the club. Said the day before he'd met a man who claimed he worked here and needed to get a message to us that he was OK. He was trying to help at the Convention Center. Keep peace. Keep people alive, I guess. Then he heard about a lady who was six, eight blocks away, dying without her oxygen. Apparently Charlie went running around like crazy trying to find some. Trying everything to keep her alive."

She let go of my hand long enough to wipe her eyes.

"The officer—"

"Frank?"

"That's right." She seemed embarrassed by the admission that Frank had known, too.

"Frank said he saw the man twelve hours later carrying the woman down the street in water up to his chest. He was pushing through the water. Calling for help. And Lord, it was *hot*. The man, your father, got the woman to Frank's arms at the curb of the Convention Center and then laid down on the grass around the corner. Frank raced that woman to the airport where they had a little hospital set up. When Frank came back to check on your father, he was still lying flat on the grass. Only now, your father, my Charles, had a handwritten sign on his chest."

Jezebel's tears streamed all the way down her neck.

"A sign?"

"It said, SAVED A WOMAN'S LIFE."

CHAPTER

29

Jordan was stunned by the photos.

The three of us sat in my apartment, clicking one at a time through the albums on my laptop. Jordan couldn't keep her mouth closed. "I've never . . . I've never seen . . ." She hadn't finished a sentence in ten minutes.

I clicked on the group shot Frank had snapped on the street the day we took the johnboat to Dad's house in the Lower Ninth.

Jordan stared intently. "Who's that?"

I named everyone in the photo.

"The girl next to you—is that Bela?"

"Uh, yeah, Bela Cruz, how'd you know?"

"You must have mentioned her," Jordan said.

I hadn't noticed earlier just how close Bela and I were standing in the photo.

Jez excused herself to the bathroom.

Jordan noticed.

"Tell me about her," she said.

"Not much to tell." I hated lying to my best friend. "She's a grad student, worked at the club. She helped with recovery."

Jordan studied the photo then put her hand on my cheek. "You know what I see in this photo, Luke?"

"What?"

"A look I'm unfamiliar with."

"I'm lost."

"No, you're not. That look on your face . . ." She gently guided my chin toward the screen on my laptop so I couldn't look in any other direction. "I've never seen that look before."

We both knew exactly what she meant. Jordan rarely cried, but her eyes were unmistakably wet.

She stared back at my face in the photo. "I've waited to see that look since our first date."

"IHOP."

"Belgian waffles." She took my hand.

I kissed the back of hers.

"I'm your best friend, Luke, and heaven and all my girlfriends know I've wanted to be more. But Luke, girls know looks."

What do I say?

"You're stuck, aren't you?"

I nodded my head ever so slightly.

"Oh, Luke. I've known our visions of this haven't been the same."

"How?"

She closed the laptop and took my other hand, too. "Did you fall in love with me the first time we met?"

I looked past her and out the window.

"Luke, the first time you saw me—that first meeting—*did you know?*"

I didn't have to answer. *Was this my father's final lesson?*

"Luke." Her wet eyes couldn't hold the tears up any longer. "That look on your face says you've *got* to find her."

"I'm not sure I can."

"Yes, you can."

"How do you know?"

"I told you—the *look*." She stood up and put her arms around my shoulders. "And I guess I just have a feeling."

Premonition.

Jordan pulled a Kleenex from her purse, wiped her nose, then kissed me on the cheek again.

Jezebel stepped back into the room with her arms crossed in front of her chest and her head bowed slightly.

"Thank you, Jezebel," Jordan said the words so sweetly, so sincerely, as if they'd known each other for years.

"You're welcome." She said the words as she stepped in for a tight hug. Then, as she let go of Jordan, Jez placed her hands on her red cheeks.

"You're going to be OK."

"I know," she said.

"Come see me sometime?" Jez asked, and most wouldn't have meant it.

"Mm-hmm," Jordan answered.

"Be safe." Jez kissed her forehead and retreated quietly to the kitchen.

"Please call," Jordan said to me. "When you're back. When your father is settled. Please."

"I will."

"Promise?"

"Of course. You're still the best friend I've ever had."

She hugged me again. "I love you, Luke."

"I know. I love you, too. I always will."

She put the Kleenex back to her eyes and walked toward the door.

"Good-bye," I said.

"Not good-bye," she said, looking over her shoulder.

I think she wanted to say something else, but instead she blew me a kiss, smiled, and shut the door behind her.

Jez reemerged. "I'm sorry," she said.

"It's OK. She'll never be out of my life. I couldn't afford to lose her." I'd said that before, but never with much sincerity. It felt good to mean it this time.

"What's next?" Jez asked.

"Pack your bag back up. I've got to run to the basement and then we're off."

"Now?"

"Now."

"All right," she said.

"Let's get my father to Texas."

I didn't wait for the elevator. Despite sore, achy legs, I ran down fourteen flights of stairs to the basement with the key to my storage closet clutched in my fist.

I opened the metal door and rummaged for the last package Dad had sent me. It was bigger than I remembered when it first arrived.

I jabbed and cut through the packing tape with the key and dug through the foam peanuts.

I slowly pulled out a case, and my heart raced exactly the way I'd expected.

I set the case on the floor and unlatched the lid.

A saxophone with a tiny wrinkle in the bell.

I could barely see it through the tears.

I lifted it from the red-velvet-lined case.

I held it in my hands like a newborn and wept.

In the case I also found a folded, handwritten chord chart to a song Dad had started but not finished. He'd called it "Love Me if You Can."

Just to the side of the title, he'd scribbled the words:

HELP ME WRITE MY SECOND VERSE, SON.

CHAPTER

30

Four days later, FEMA transferred Dad's body to Dallas. It helped that one of Dad's old partners at the firm was from Crawford, Texas.

The funeral was scheduled for a Saturday, a day when many from Dad's old firm promised they could attend. I was humbled by how many kept their word.

Lee, Dad's very first A.A. sponsor from Austin, made the trip. So did a half-dozen others from Step Eight on Dad's list.

We bypassed a traditional church service and opted to hold all the services graveside. It had been a week since Jez had shown up at my doorstep, and she hadn't left my side. I liked being at her side.

I'd initially asked Jordan to come—and she wanted to—but when she told me one of the biggest deals of her career was collapsing at home in New York, I uninvited her.

"You're sure?" she asked me on the phone. "It's just work. You're a bazillion times more important."

"Of course I'm sure," I answered. "You don't have to be here for me to know you care."

"Dinner when you get back?"

"Of course," I said. I knew she was curious to know whether I'd found Bela, but I also knew she wasn't ready to ask. *In time,* I thought.

Since first arriving back home, I'd called Jerome dozens of times trying to find her.

"Still nothin'," he said each time. "No one has seen her, son."

Jez assumed she was home in Arizona. A good guess, but her last name, Cruz, was like looking for a grain of salt in a desert sand dune. We'd come up empty.

"Appropriate," I told Jez. "Empty is exactly how I feel without her here to help bury my father."

The service was short. I spoke, Jez said a few quick words, and Dad's confidant and most loyal friend, Kaiser, added some thoughtful words about the man Dad had been, the man he fell into, and the man he'd become at death.

No more inspired words were ever spoken.

After Dad's former secretary offered a brief benediction, the emotional crowd of twenty-eight stood to pay their final respects.

But the sound of a vehicle pulled our attention to the cemetery's southern hillside.

First the white top crested the hill. Then the grill. Then the rest of the only fifteen-passenger van I'd ever ridden in.

The name Verses was painted on both sides.

Jez stepped up to me and put both her arms through one of mine. "Oh, my! A funeral march!" I think she'd meant to whisper.

They parked Jesse a hundred yards away and unloaded. Jerome, Tater, Hamp, Castle, and a woman Castle carried in his arms and placed in a wheelchair—his cancer-surviving sister.

From behind the van appeared one more mourner. Even from a distance the figure's legs were bronze and beautiful, the hair gorgeous. It blew behind her in a gentle breeze as if God Himself were tousling it. She wore a white spring dress and twirled a purple parasol. I felt enough sparks to start a bonfire.

They took their instruments from their cases and played "Just a Closer Walk with Thee" as they marched toward the grave like a classic New Orleans jazz funeral. They were ragtag no more. They played the clarinet, bass drum, tuba, and the same trombone and trumpet I'd seen in New Awlins.

For a moment there was no Katrina, no recovery, no helicopters, no Guardsmen to tell the holdouts where to go or when to go home.

No politics. No hearings. No fraud, waste, or blame.

Just a funeral dirge the way only the people of New Orleans could perform it.

When they got closer, they "cut the body loose" and broke

into the traditional "Second Line." Joyful riffs, smiling, voices, and chords in celebration.

Lastly, the funeral march played the tune to a song I'd only ever seen on paper in Dad's handwriting: "Love Me if You Can."

The band played the first verse while Bela sang Dad's letter-perfect lyrics.

After the crowd cleared, Bela and I sat on the grass near Dad's grave and wrote his second verse.

Together.

"Love Me if You Can"

Tonight I tried to write the perfect song of love
But all the words I sang were blue
Because I've tried and I've tried to win you over
And I've done the best I can do
So we may never be together
But my heart is in your hands
And if you ever think about me in your long-lost dreams
Love me if you can

I know that you've moved on, it's what you had to do
I never had the chance to say good-bye
It's on my list of all the things I never said
It goes on for pages and it keeps me up at night
And my heart is missing pieces
That only you could understand
So if you ever think about it in your long-lost dreams
Love me if you can

So this song I sing is a little sad
And it's unrehearsed
I just hope you hear that this broken life
Has had a second verse

'Cause in those days gone by, I tried to build you castles
And maybe they just turned to sand
But if you can only love who you wished I could have been
I wish you knew it's finally who I am
I remember how you needed me
And I know yesterday will never come again
But if you feel me reaching for you in your long-lost dreams
Love me if you can

Listen to the song at www.RecoveringCharles.com

ACKNOWLEDGMENTS

My eternal thanks go to the usual suspects: My four children, my three siblings, my two parents, and my one and only best friend and wife, Kodi.

Thanks also to my early-draft reviewers—Allyson, Ann, Becky, Christa, Cindy, Jane, Jeanette, Kalley, Larry, Laura, Laurel, Laurie, Matt, Nancy, Randa—and specifically to Chrissy Funk for her fine work as a research assistant and to Bill Roach for being my New Orleans friend and guru. Special thanks also to Cherie Call for lending her incredible songwriting talents. You're a gem.

You wouldn't be holding this book if not for the creative and brave souls at Shadow Mountain: Chris Schoebinger, Lisa Mangum, Richard Erickson, Sheryl Dickert Smith, Gail Halladay, Angie Godfrey, Tiffany Williams, Patrick Muir, Jamie Barrett, Erin Crouse, Tonya Facemyer, Natalie Bellamy, Laurel Christensen, Chrislyn Barnes, Sharon Larsen, Laurie Sumsion, Boyd Ware, John Rose, Lonnie Lockhart, Lee Broadhead, Keith Hunter, Jeff

Simpson, Pat Williams, and last, but certainly not least, Sheri Dew.

Once again I'm grateful to York and Laura Faulkner for their tremendous generosity. We'd have peace on earth if everyone spent just one night at *Harmony Woods*. I also thank the wonderful folks at the Holiday Inn Express, Woodstock, Virginia. (I owe you a towel.)

I'm extremely grateful for the support and patience of my fellow Church members in Woodstock, Virginia, especially my long-suffering students: Bryan, Caleb, Glen, Matt, Michael, Olivia, and Spencer. Thanks also to the Shenandoah Valley Chapter of the Mandate Association. (See you on the 4th Wednesday.)

Thanks to my literary agent, Laurie Liss, for having faith.

Most importantly, thanks to the people of New Orleans for taking Mother Nature's best hit and standing tall. You paid a tremendous price to remind us all that America is still the loving, generous country the Founders dreamt of.

May God watch over your long-term recovery.